PRINTZ

PRINTZ

Maryann D'Agincourt

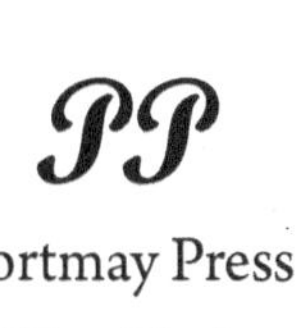

Portmay Press
New York

Design and typesetting by Patricia Fabricant.
FRONT COVER: Amedeo Modigliani, *Portrait of Henri Laurens, sitting*, 1915, Rosengart Collection Museum Lucerne
BACK COVER: Willem de Kooning, *Seated Woman*, c. 1940. Philadelphia Museum of Art, The Albert M. Greenfield and Elizabeth M. Greenfield Collection. Object Number 1974-178-23.

Printed in the United States of America
First published in 2017 by Portmay Press, New York
This paperback edition published in 2019 by Portmay Press, New York

ISBN 978-0-9994006-6-1 (pb)

Publisher's Cataloging-in-Publication
(Provided by Quality Books, Inc.)
D'Agincourt, Maryann, author.
Printz / Maryann D'Agincourt.
pages cm
ISBN 978-0-9891745-9-6
1. Grief--Fiction. 2. Man-woman relationships--Fiction. 3. Life change events--France--Paris--Fiction. 4. Moving, Household--United States--Fiction. 5. Brothers and sisters--Fiction. 6. Psychological fiction. I. Title.
PS3604.A332544P75 2017 813'.6
QBI17-900042

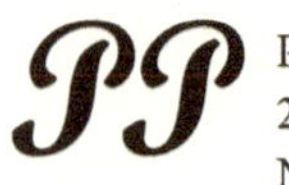

Portmay Press
244 Madison Avenue
New York, NY 10016
www.portmaypress.com

For Greg

With deep gratitude to Emily Albarillo—
a wonderfully gifted editor

"We all need a past—that's where our sense of identity comes from."

—Penelope Lively

"We are minor in everything but our passions."

—Elizabeth Bowen

Late October

A flutist's rendering of "Good Morning Heartache," coming from a CD playing in the neighboring apartment, filters in while Jacob and Greta breakfast in their cramped kitchen. As it is early, outside there is more darkness than light. Immune to the sound of the flute, Jacob is preoccupied with what he's about to ask her, what will be a question of no apparent significance. But Greta pauses and listens attentively to the faint music. With the exception of a slight smile crossing her lips, her expression is still.

A lone branch scrapes against the pane of the curtainless window; on the sill and around the rectangular frame the paint is cracked and chipping. The kitchen flooring, covered with black-and-white linoleum tiles, is uneven, lower near the sink and raised beneath the window. Above the table, one bulb, housed in a cratered brass fixture hanging from the ceiling, emits a soft light. There is a reflection of Jacob, the slope of his shoulders, in the glass door of the cabinet. Greta wears fitted woolen pants and a pale yellow sweater that enhances her slightly ruddy complexion. With ease she leans forward, one wrist against the edge of the table, a fork in her other hand, taking light, neat stabs at her omelet before breaking off a piece to eat.

Because of his height, which he's found to be more of an annoyance than an attribute—six foot three—Jacob sits to the side with his legs crossed. He's dressed in a gray suit, a cream-colored shirt, and a beige tie with the imprint of a leaf in the center. When he finishes eating he frowns, and with mild frustration, as if it's been blocking his view, he pushes his dish to the side. He looks across the table at Greta. She chews with her lips tightly closed, her chin-length hair covering much of her face. He waits, and when she looks up, their gazes meet; he is struck as always by the fine streaks of gold in her brown eyes and he experiences a brief sense of renewal, but soon uneasiness descends. He clears his throat then speaks in an exacting voice—a tone of his he knows she's not familiar with—as he tells her Royce Wagner, his friend from college, will stop by today, late in the afternoon. Would she like to meet Royce? She nods, her expression softening, and continues eating. He is reassured, but soon feels a slight tug in his chest as he does whenever he mentions Royce to her, and also because at this moment she is both fully present and only a shadow of herself.

Jacob deftly uncrosses his legs, then gets up to pour himself more coffee; placing the cup on the counter, he loosely picks up the pot. Greta puts down her fork, leans back in her chair and, with a caring dispassion, she studies him. His chestnut-colored hair is parted to the side, his mustache partially covers his upper lip; he repeatedly brings one finger from his free hand to his mouth as if to brush back the whiskers—a reflex she has not taken note of until now. Back at the table, he abruptly stirs the teaspoon of sugar he's put into his cup. His fixed expression reveals how conflicted he is.

In the ten months she's known Jacob, she's found him to be for the most part responsive and considerate, yet she is not fully comfortable living with him. It is something she refuses to dwell on for too long; if she were to ponder their involvement too much, question it, she believes in some way she will lose part of herself, a part of herself she has not yet defined or perhaps even unearthed. Her acceptance of her unsettled feelings for him has become part of the tempo of their relationship. And because of this she is not diverted by the change in his tone this morning or that he does not seem like himself. Usually grinning and assured in a self-deprecating way, today he is instead somber, restless.

Their age difference—thirteen years—creates, she believes, a certain mystery between them and because of it at times they listen more closely to each other, though in certain instances, they listen not at all. Whenever their relationship is too much for Greta, too much for her to bear, she will, for a multitude of reasons, recall Tommaso. Thinking of Tommaso lessens any doubts she may have about Jacob, about how much older he is.

And for a reason she cannot fathom, paradoxical perhaps, recalling Tommaso makes her less jittery—since her time in Europe last year she's become more so in a way she's not been before.

She now looks toward the window, eyes the scraping branch, how it zigzags across the pane, its hypnotic motion inducing her to last night, Jacob coming toward her as she lay in bed, her nightgown unbuttoned. His gaze was warm, but then he sat on the edge of the mattress close to her and without a trace of his usual spontaneity, he bent over, wrapping his arms round her. She felt the stiff and unyielding pressure of his chest against her breasts. Slowly she freed herself from his embrace. His dark eyes became distant. Turning away from him, her sight rested on the painting on the wall next to his side of the bed. It was a framed print of de Kooning's *Seated Woman*. There had been a copy of the same painting in the townhouse outside of Paris they'd stayed in ten months before. She assumed he'd ordered a replica for their present apartment as a memento of their time together in France, but after living with him for nearly a year she's instead realized its significance for him is a vague mystery to her. When he noticed her looking at the copy of the painting he began to massage her shoulders, his expression pleading, his eyes more caring; she knew he hoped to draw her attention, or maybe his own, from it.

She now looks away from the window, reaches for a piece of toast, and hears him tapping the toe of his shoe on the linoleum-tiled floor. "Greta?" he asks. "Do you remember the photos I showed you of Royce?" Brusquely leaning forward, he sounds unabashedly inquisitive, almost pressured, she thinks.

Mildly puzzled, she nods, catching a flicker of nervousness in his eyes, but immediately he looks away, at the clock above the stove. She recalls that December evening ten months ago; snowbound in a high-ceilinged townhouse in a Paris suburb, they'd known each other for only a few days. One night after dinner they had placed two sofa cushions on the floor before the French doors; then, sipping wine, they looked out at the falling snow. Adroitly, Jacob dug into his back pants pocket and took out an old phone he still carried with him. Smiling and lightly shaking his head, his face unshaven, he showed her two photos of Royce: one taken a few years before at a party—Jacob in the background and Royce up front, holding up a mug of beer that covered much of his face—and then there was another one, a photo of an old photo of Jacob and Royce as college freshmen standing arm in arm with other students in front of a brick wall. Neither picture had given her a sense of Royce's appearance. In the more recent photo, his features were blurred and mostly hidden, and in the other picture his face was in the distance, still without definition. What she could determine from those two photos of Royce was that he was very blond-looking next to Jacob. She had no sense of his demeanor, facial features, or physical self, other than that he was shorter than Jacob—by how much she was not able to tell.

Jacob looks back at her, his lips curling into a hopeful smile. He takes a last sip of coffee from his cup.

Once Jacob leaves for work, she is on edge from the stillness surrounding her, a stillness reminiscent of her childhood. To distract herself, she places the cups and plates in the dishwasher and then makes the bed. After picking up a red embroidered pillow she straightens her posture and eyes the copy of the de Kooning. Piqued and compelled, she drops the pillow onto the bed and stands before the copy with her arms crossed, studying it with a piercing curiosity. But the figure appears flat and uninteresting in the cold morning light.

Although Friday is her day off, Greta decides to go in to work. For the last six months she's been the manager of a children's bookshop in Harvard Square, specializing in literature, mostly from Europe. On quiet days, she'll go into the office with a book that has caught her attention and peruse the colorful and artful illustrations.

A cold, drizzly rain falls as she makes her way across Harvard Yard. The shop is a ten-minute walk from the apartment. It is still quite early and so there is very little activity, a few students and others, like Greta, on their way to work, walking through the square.

Sidney, the graduate student she's hired to work two afternoons and one full day a week, is surprised to see her come in on her day off. He is thin and not very tall; his expression more often than not is solemn and abstracted. He asks if she is okay. She nods. His gaze lingers on her as if he is waiting for her to tell him what is on her mind. She remains silent and he soon lowers his eyes and continues unpacking a large shipment of books from Helsinki that arrived late in the afternoon yesterday.

"I'll be here for a few hours. I need to review the accounts. Hilda wants to go over them with me on Monday. I forgot to check them yesterday," she says apologetically. Hilda, the woman who owns the shop, lives most of the year in Paris, and she will only allow Greta to work on the accounts from the computer in the store.

"Fine, Greta," he says curtly, not looking up, now intent on unpacking the books before opening the store for the day.

Alone in her small, almost tidy office, Greta covers her face with her hands and begins to sob. It is the first time in her life she cries for no concrete reason.

Jacob locks his car door, the cold, damp autumn air tightening his exposed hands. He strides across the community college parking lot, thrashing through a pile of fallen leaves before stopping to gaze up at the naked trees. A sharp wind brushes past him and he moves on. He's bothered about having Greta meet Royce. His presence may elicit certain memories for her. Late yesterday afternoon Royce had called unexpectedly to say he'd be in town for the weekend. Jacob waited until morning to tell Greta—he had not wanted to preoccupy her with news of his friend. Yesterday was her birthday.

He opens the door to the room that serves as both his office and classroom, then switches on the lights. Standing before his desk, he unlocks the top drawer, opens it, and takes out a photo of Catherine. His heart beats quickly. It was taken about five years ago, before she moved to the West Coast; she is wearing a yellow-and-rose-colored halter dress. Jacob had asked to take her picture, telling her it was because he wanted to test his new camera. When she turned to him and said, "Sure," he had snapped the photo. It captures her restiveness as well as her fondness for him. He never showed her the photo, nor did he show it to anyone else. Now he does what he does every morning—he holds it close to his face and in a priestly way he kisses her forehead. Lowering the photo, he catches his reflection in the windowpane; his expression is both surly and pained—this startles him. He puts the photo back into the drawer and locks it. Then, noticing the date on the desk calendar, he becomes slightly agitated—in less than a week it will be a year since his life began to unravel.

The previous November and December

A longing to be at the center of activity had guided Jacob Printz throughout much of his adult life—his striving to be there had been like pulling on a rope in a tug of war; it had always been that rigorous for him. For he had believed he needed to be wherever that pulse of activity emanated from to keep his life and humor intact. But one stark November day, leaving Catherine's hospital room, his eyes heavy from lack of sleep, he was shaky and uncertain. Moments before, he'd stood at the foot of Catherine's bed and had observed his sister, unconscious and surrounded by tubes, wires, and machines. Everything was white—her face, the sheets, the walls, the water pitcher, the sink, even the vase of calla lilies he'd sent. His mind went blank. For on the deepest possible level he understood the center, whether it be social or philosophical, was most likely an illusion after all.

He'd last seen Catherine only a few months earlier. She'd come for a short visit to their parents' home in Philadelphia. It had been a breezy September afternoon with a strong sun.

"Where have you been?" she had cried out, turning her head toward the door when he first walked in. She sat slouched on the sofa, strips of light covering her legs stretched out across an ottoman, a magazine on her lap. She had just flown in from the West Coast. Jacob had been working for thirty days straight on a campaign in the western part of the state. Exhausted, he had put down his suitcase.

Her shoulder-length pale hair was lightly tangled, he noticed, and her lipstick a little smudged. Slim and long-legged, she was dressed in a short black skirt, black tights, a pink T-shirt, and he'd thought of licorice, sweet and twisty. But her tone was firm, not sugary—she told him he looked tired, that he was driving himself too hard, that he was neglecting her.

After lecturing him, she sprang up from the sofa, went over and hugged him, laughing. Then he felt the pressure of her hand, small for her height, on his chest as she said, her voice now mellifluent, "Jake, it's always great to see you," her eyes avoiding his gaze.

"You too, Catherine," he answered hesitantly. He was dubious of her mood and, as usual, his heart beat more quickly the way it did whenever she stood close to him.

Just as Catherine turned away, the doorbell rang. "That's Royce," he said tersely.

"Royce," she repeated; she nervously patted down her hair with her hands, then straightened her skirt. Raising her head, she said, "Your friend from college, the one you'd always talk about, but for some unknown and mysterious reason you never invited here?"

"Royce Wagner—and I have today," he answered curtly.

She eyed him, inhaling, her nose pinched, as if she'd had surgery to narrow it, but she hadn't—it had always looked that way, even when she was a young girl. "Let him in," she said coaxingly, drawing back her head.

Soon Royce, who was six inches shorter than Jacob, was hugging him. But once they separated, Jacob noted an expression of mild surprise crossing his friend's face. Following his gaze, he saw that Royce was looking at Catherine, his blue-green eyes slightly narrowing. When he introduced Catherine to Royce, she had been subdued.

Before he'd turned to leave the hospital room, he thought he saw a flicker of movement cross her face. Had she raised her eyebrows the way she used to whenever she'd say goodbye to him? He moved closer, lowering his face to hers. The beauty spot above the bridge of her nose had looked more pronounced against the whiteness of her skin. He'd pursed his lips and blew across her face, hoping to awaken her, as if they were in a fairy tale. But her expression was as still and bland as it had been for the last few days, her eyebrows dull and wispy—the only movement had been that of his imagination.

Now striding down the hallway, he passed the nurse's station without a glance, his hands dug deep in the pockets of his raincoat. He hadn't had a drink in days, and that was what he most needed now.

Once the elevator door opened to the lobby, he heard familiar voices coming from the waiting area. His parents' voices were lower pitched and more rounded than usual but as dissonant to him, because of the persistent rhythm of their speech, as the parakeets he'd heard as a child at the tropical resort they'd often visited in the Caribbean.

In their late sixties, his mother and father, Leah Lane and Maxwell Printz, carried themselves as if they were ten or fifteen years younger. His father was dressed in a navy blue tailored suit and matching tie, his brown hair brushed to the side, graying at the temples. And although it was past eight in the evening, his mother, in a black suede coat, wore dark glasses, her blond hair held back in a ponytail.

"Jacob," his father called out, his voice hoarse with worry. His mother sat on a straight-backed chair, her hands clasped on her lap, her face down. But once he approached, she raised her head and took off her sunglasses. He noticed how red her eyes were. His father embraced him. In her pointed way, his mother asked, "Do you know exactly what happened, Jake? You've been the closest to Cate, you know her best."

"It was an accident, plain and simple," he said, bending down to kiss her, knowing she had asked because she was looking for some sort of reassurance; she knew as much about what had happened to Catherine as he did. Up close she appeared slightly older, more tired, and so did his father. It crossed his mind that maybe what had befallen Catherine in some way had been their fault. If they had been more attentive to her when she was young. . . . Yet even as Jacob considered this, he knew it wasn't that straightforward. In his eyes, Catherine had always been capricious. But this had been an accident—another driver had swerved to the wrong side of the road, slamming into her car. It had had nothing to do with her temperament.

"Yes, Jake," his mother said, bringing her forefinger to her bottom lip, "but I believe what happened to Cate isn't just an accident—life is far too complicated. It's difficult to digest, to understand." Her lips were dry, her mouth barely open; it was as if it were nearly frozen, tears trickling down the sides of her face. She put the sunglasses on again and Jacob caught, wafting from the inner part of her narrow wrists, the musky scent of her perfume.

For an hour he walked about the city in a numbed state. Philadelphia was different that night, he thought, looking up at the tall buildings, many with lights on, the dark sky, a backdrop. The very same structures he had been impressed with as a teen now appeared unfamiliar and distant. It was as if he were a stranger, as if he had never been there before, or as if in some way Philadelphia had rejected him.

He remembered the bar he had gone to with Royce and Catherine that September night. As he took a left onto Third Street, the wind lashed his neck. He gulped the cold air, then opened the door and stepped inside. He went over to the table where the three of them had sat. It was unoccupied. He touched the shiny surface with his cold, red hand and stared down at the table as if in doing so he would be transported back to that night.

Catherine had sat with them for a little over an hour. Out of the corner of his eye as he had turned away to signal the waiter for another round of drinks, he thought he saw Catherine, just returning from the restroom, hand a sticky note to Royce. But when he was again facing them, she reached out and touched his shoulder with her hand and said, "I must go, Jake."

Now he shook his head and went over to the bar and sat on a stool. A few seats over from him, he noticed a woman in her late thirties, close to his age. She appeared somewhat familiar. But that would often happen, he came across so many people in his work, traveling around with candidates who were running for governor or the senate or state senate. There were always faces that looked familiar in a crowd. And he'd investigate each one, ask where he or she was from. For he usually mingled with the crowd before and after a candidate's speech to discover what people were thinking, what issues were most important to them. But each time, the more he'd converse with one of those familiar faces, the more unfamiliar he or she would become.

Thirty minutes or so later the woman came and sat next to him. She must have noticed him looking at her. Now dissociated from drinking, he no longer remembered she had at first appeared to be someone he knew. He could not see her clearly. But soon he turned to her and said, a little too exuberantly, "Well, hello, there!" At this point he was beyond caring how loud he might sound. The liquor was surging through him, bolstering him. And he was his old self.

"Are you Jacob Printz?" she asked. Her face seemed hazy.

He nodded, and said, "You must know me through my work."

She shook her head and said, "No, I don't know about your work. I know you from a long time ago."

He didn't hear her words—his mind was numb. But he perceived kindness in her, in the way her shoulder leaned toward him, and openness in her broad, high forehead. Kindness was something he had not experienced much of, even with Catherine. Catherine, yes, he thought. And tears rushed to his eyes. Through his watery gaze, he saw that the woman was turning away. When she swiveled back toward him, she handed him a handkerchief. Grasping it, he rolled it into a ball and dabbed his eyes. That was the last thing he remembered.

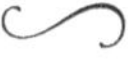

When he awoke the next morning, he found himself alone in a strange room. His head hurt so much he could barely lift it from the pillow. He hadn't had that much to drink in a very long while, and as the pain sliced through his head, he remembered why he had stopped. But when he thought of Catherine lying in the hospital bed with all those tubes and machines close to her, he wished he had not awakened.

Everything seemed close, even the pale yellow walls of this small room and the white bureau and bookcase—more white, he agonized, and knew he needed to leave immediately. Then he remembered the woman at the bar and realized she must have brought him home with her. He closed his eyes, trying to recall what she looked like, but his mind drew a blank.

He must see Catherine again, he thought, feeling a wrenching sense of panic.

He heard a knock at the door. "Yes," he said, angry he did not know where he was.

The woman opened the door; he was able to clearly see her face. And then he groaned. She'd been a classmate of his in high school, a quiet, studious type. What was her name—Salte was her last name, and he'd heard she'd gone to medical school, but that was years ago. That was all he could recall about her.

As she stood before him in the light of day she no longer seemed shy, but confident, more attractive than he'd remembered, her long fine hair now cut short, nicely framing her face. And despite her apparent poise, for some reason he felt sorry for her. But he was empty. "I need to go," he said brusquely.

On the thirtieth of November, Greta Hatler arrived at Gare de Lyon at four in the afternoon, the eleven-hour train ride from Florence having passed with the fitfulness and haze of a dream. Throughout the journey, she had sat erectly, her hands, ash white, clasped tightly on her lap, her worn backpack with a partially broken zipper in the empty seat next to her, her toes jostling together from the vibrations of the engine. She had only looked forward, barely taking note of the snow-crowned Alps or the brown fields and gated farmhouses along the route.

Now rolling her suitcase through the maze and ruckus of the Paris train station, she was flooded with images from the previous day—a cold morning, sitting in a café with eleven others, all women, waiting for Tommaso, the belt of the professor's trenchcoat soiled from a puddle of water she had walked through; Tommaso smoking in the dark, Florentine night, leaning against the wrought-iron railing of the restaurant they'd just left.

At last, stepping outside Gare de Lyon, she felt a breeze. It was a surprisingly soft afternoon. The sky was a light, puffy gray. Two women and two men, all four of them in tight-fitted suits, walked swiftly past as she moved toward the curb. Raising her hand to hail a taxi, she felt the weight of Tommaso's ring on her left forefinger, a gold ring with what might be a family crest of some sort, one she could not decipher, something she had not asked him about, though it evoked a semblance of sophistication and grandeur.

The cab was warm and roomy with smooth leather seats. She handed the driver a note card with the address of the hotel. His face was narrow, his hair dark, close to his head. As he studied it, she pressed her palm against the soft seat. Then he looked back at her, gave her the card and turned away, nodding. Efficiently, he said, "*Merci*."

"*Merci*," she repeated, but as she was unfamiliar with the language, she thought her execution awkward, her tone flat.

As they drove through the streets, despite the time of year, she noticed a lightness she'd not experienced in Florence, a city swirling with the ghosts of the Medici family, the centuries-past burning of Savonarola in the piazza outside the Palazzo Vecchio, and echoing images of Dante. And then there had been her own strict and complicated passion for Tommaso.

The boulevard was lined with tall buildings mostly pale gray, nearly blending with the sky, a few adorned with colorful flags. She raised her hand and bent her forefinger, grazing Tommaso's ring against her cheek, thinking that only twenty-four hours earlier, they had been at the Uffizi Gallery, the last class, the twelve of them, including the instructor. Beth Rogers, who had arranged the three-month session in Florence, had been their art history professor in college. They had agreed to go to Italy because none of them had had any other plans.

Greta recalled Tommaso standing before Titian's *Venus of Urbino*. Grinning, he had drawn a handkerchief from his pocket, then dropping his right shoulder forward, holding the cloth in that hand, crossing his knees, he languidly lowered his left hand. Given that he was upright, he was doing his best to imitate Venus's pose. Even the professor laughed, her eyes glistening behind the lenses of her tortoise-rimmed glasses, her head thrust back. She approved of Tommaso; she had invited him to join their group when she'd met him the previous year in Florence.

Greta knew, as did the others, even those least dazzled by the great works surrounding them, that as Tommaso gracefully and adroitly mimicked Venus, he was not mocking the art, but chiding their American perspective, not natural or sensual, too academic, too forced, he'd say repeatedly. Greta knew her professor was as compelled by him as she was, his freedom from inhibitions, his naturalness, his innate lack of caution. "You Americans, you are sensually stiff, you must let yourself go with art—with everything," he'd repeat as one might recite the opening line of a favorite novel. Although he was only a year or two older, he diminished in every way the men she'd known in college. They had not been as indulgent as Tommaso, touching only when necessary—for a hollow pleasure alone—as they preferred sex quick and over with, wanting to get on with things. And most often the humor those men subscribed to was laced not with irony but with sarcasm.

She now pressed her fingers over her eyes, swollen from crying. She thought of the dinner the night before at the small restaurant with beige corrugated wallpaper and black iron shields hanging about the room. All twelve of them had sat at a long wooden table near the foyer—she next to Tommaso, his knee pressing her leg. Across from him was Elaine, her deep brown eyes thoughtful; she chewed a strand of her hair as she studied him. And then to Greta's right, Patty, short-cropped hair and a wide smile, restless in her chair, teasing him about his recent haircut. At the head of the table sat Professor Beth Rogers, downing her third glass of wine.

Greta thought of the three of them because she believed they were the ones who were as taken with Tommaso as she was. The others found him too Italian, too foreign, and she knew that although they appreciated to a certain degree their time in Italy, they longed to return home to the expansiveness of Chicago, the brisk pace of New York, or the predictability of New England, and their plainspoken families.

After the meal, Tommaso sat back in the chair and pulled out a cigar. With a broad smile, he told them they would miss Italy, the food, the drink, the *passione*. His face was flushed from the wine, his blue-green eyes impish. With a quick movement of his hand he brushed back his brown-streaked blond hair. Everyone laughed, even those who had not found him absorbing. But instead Greta had been saddened; she thought how Italy had loosened something within her, as if she'd been embraced by a warm and fierce wind—and now she was leaving.

The taxi driver took a left onto a side street in Saint-Germain-des-Prés and pulled up in front of a hotel. She paid him, and he sped off. Alone, clutching the handle of her suitcase, about to roll it inside, she looked up at the building, four stories high, a light pink with mauve-colored shutters on the windows, quaint-looking on the narrow street. She felt vaguely hopeful.

Once she was settled in her room, she opened the window and was met with a quick sharp breeze. She gazed down the street at an antique store with a gold inlaid table in the window. Then she saw a group of people on the sidewalk below, casually walking, laughing. She shut the window, then turned away and looked around the room, taking note of the burgundy-colored wallpaper with tiny white flowers, the lace curtains, and the doilies scattered across the top of the bureau.

When her cell phone rang, she froze, her heart beating

rapidly. The space was small, the bed large; she awkwardly walked to the other side of the room, where she'd put down her phone, her knees bumping against the footboard. As she reached to pick up the cell, she saw her mother's name and number—she was most likely calling to let her know when her plane would be landing the next day. They had communicated mostly through emails and had last spoken on Greta's birthday in late October. She was comforted by the thought that her mother would soon be with her. After Tommaso, she needed her mother's unflappable presence, something she'd not desired in a long while. Greta looked forward to relaying all that had happened in Florence, and she knew that in her practical way her mother would dampen her imagination, allay her fears.

As they exchanged greetings, Greta tightly held the phone, and pictured her mother in jeans and a loose gray sweatshirt, at the kitchen window, impassively looking out at the now-bare maple tree. Or maybe she was standing in front of the TV, listening to the news. But Greta believed she most likely was in the bedroom, her back to Greta's father, who would be sitting up in bed, fully dressed—it was midday there and he'd be home from the shop for a few hours—his back against the headboard, reading the news from his iPad.

Greta's parents, Geraldine and Mark Hatler, had been art majors at the University of Massachusetts. They had left Springfield, Massachusetts, thirty-five years before to move close to Boston, purchasing a card shop on a gritty main street in a suburb just south of the city, ever present was the lingering smell of the ocean. They sold cards with prints of many of their own original designs on the front, mostly abstract and some copies from works of well-known artists—Renoir's *Dance at Bougival* was one of her mother's favorites—surprisingly, as Greta had not thought her to be particularly romantic. And there was a print of herself at ten—she had posed for her mother. Using watercolors, Geraldine had painted a picture of Greta wearing a large straw hat with flowers springing out from the band, real ones, similar in theme to a work of Renoir. Greta recalled how the brim of the hat had rubbed against her forehead, and her mother's stare as she painted, exacting and solemn. How severely disappointed Greta had been when she eventually saw the print of it on the front of the cards. She believed it wasn't close to how she had looked the day her mother had painted it or to the actual watercolor. Her familiar straight brown hair with red highlights and her tanned narrow hands grasping a red balloon, the same straw hat with flowers falling over the brim—but the flattened face, the expressionless eyes; how unlike her it was! When she had asked her mother about it, Geraldine had told her in a factual way that it was because it was a print. But Greta needed to see the original: "Where is your painting, the first one?" a ten-year-old Greta demanded. Her mother smiled slightly, a distant look in her eyes, saying she had filed it away, but one day she would find it for her. As young as she was Greta instinctively understood her mother had misplaced the original.

Even then Greta had felt estranged from her family. It was difficult now to reconcile she was the older sister of doleful Eric, and the younger sister of the inscrutable Claudine.

As she spoke to her mother, letting her know she was settled in the hotel, she heard a sigh in the background, and then a door open and shut. She realized her subtly restless father, who had a penchant for cannabis and a dislike of phone talk, must have left the room. When her mother asked her about her last days in Florence, she became excited; holding the phone to her ear with one shoulder, she stroked Tommaso's ring with her thumb, the indentations from the crest leaving marks on it. She spoke rapidly about the paintings in the Uffizi, the food and the wine, and felt her cheeks reddening.

When Greta finished, her mother remarked that it must have been a wonderful experience, her voice even yet encouraging—her way of showing her affection for her daughter. Before Greta was able to savor the care in her mother's voice, Geraldine added that her own mother was not well, and that she'd have to travel to Springfield to see her. And so she had had to cancel her trip to France. Greta felt a sinking within at the thought of her ill grandmother, the fact that she would be alone in Paris, alone with memories of Tommaso. Why had her mother waited so long to reveal the true purpose of her call, why had she allowed her to talk so profusely about her time in Italy?

Greta began to pace, told her mother she would come home immediately, that she must need her. No, Geraldine answered in a surprisingly firm voice. Stay the two weeks, stay, go to the museums, see Paris for me. When Greta didn't answer, she added in an almost wistful tone that she'd visit Paris someday, but it was not the time now. And when she hung up Greta was convinced her mother was relieved she didn't have to make the trip, that she had no inclination at all to see the Louvre or the Orsay. For she was a person who simply drew pictures or copied them.

Suddenly Greta felt weary, foggy from knowing she would not see Tommaso again, tired because of her mother's inability to come, so exhausted that, still in her clothes, she got into bed, and within minutes she fell into a deep sleep.

Her dreams were sharp and colorful. One had actually happened—it was a continuation of a memory crossing her mind before she'd dozed off. But she was unaware at what point the memory ended and the dream began:

A hot summer afternoon, the blinds have been drawn. She sits cross-legged on her cool bedroom floor, her turquoise shorts riding up her legs, an open book on her lap. Whenever she raises or lowers her head, her hair in a long, tight braid strokes her back.

Unexpectedly the door opens. She looks up and sees Eric, her ten-year-old brother, and his two friends, their heads down, avoiding her gaze. Eric's eyes are dark and contrite; he focuses on the Raggedy Ann doll on her bed as he begs her to come and play touch football with them. Readily she stands up, pleased she is a few inches taller than they are.

Outside, she catches the football, relishes the thump of the pigskin as it hits her undeveloped chest, thrilled she is physically equal to them as are most twelve-year-old girls to ten-year-old boys. She runs toward the goal line, but suddenly she is in the kitchen, nearly colliding with her mother and grandmother, who sit huddled together at the table. The football has disappeared.

Her mother turns sharply toward her, her face distorted, as if she is wearing a mask and is about to growl at Greta.

Now she is alone, standing on a sidewalk. It is very cold. So cold. She is not able to move. Tommaso saunters down the street in his brown suede jacket, his olive skin tanned. Soon she's in bed with him, they are wrapped together naked, their chests pressing together. He touches and kisses her hair, her back, her breasts, laughing warmly. But she is still; she does not return his kisses or caresses. His laughter becomes too strong, mocking. She jumps out of bed, wants to dress, but can't find her clothes. She looks in the closet, still hearing his laughter, then anxiously searches through the drawers. It is growing cold so she shuts the window, shivering.

When she gets on her knees and looks under the bed, she no longer hears Tommaso. All she sees is his ring, gold and shining in the darkness on the floor beneath the mattress. She extends her arm, hoping to grasp it, but it eludes her. She cries out his name. She blindly reaches above for the sheets or blankets to cover herself, warm herself, but nothing is on the bed—the mattress is bare. All that remains is his ring beneath the bed. Where is Tommaso? she wonders in a panic. Again, she reaches for the ring, and when she grips onto it, it stings her.

Greta awoke with a start. Not until her gaze caught the burgundy-colored wallpaper and lace curtains did she know where she was. Her eyes wet, her fists clenched, she lay curled in a fetal position—Tommaso's ring, having slipped from her finger, was scraping the palm of her hand.

Jacob was jarred by a strong gust of wind as he got out of the taxi. It was the first of December. Gloveless, he shivered, then clutched the handle of his suitcase and walked into the airport terminal. Disoriented at first by the bright lights and diffuse activity, followed by the long security line, he eventually settled into a seat at the gate, close to a desk; behind it was a screen with the flight information.

Once on the plane, tightening his seat belt, he turned his head to look out the window of the Paris-bound 747 barreling down the runway and he felt a growing sense of panic. As the jet soared upward, he eyed a few thin clouds floating by, vanishing into the night sky, much like his former life.

Markedly different from the person he'd been only months before, he could not fathom how lost he was. Each time he'd catch his reflection in a mirror, he'd notice how sunken his cheeks had become and how his effortless grin had inverted into an indelible frown. His inability to express himself as he had in the past was what he found most unsettling, more so than his grief. Although inexorably painful, wrapping himself in his grief, believing that in some way he must be dead like Catherine, had become for him a means of escape from the present, from coming to terms with this new emerging life of his.

He reached up to press the light button above his seat and noticed his hand shaking. Since Catherine's accident he had avoided the dark—for it reinforced his impression that the last half year had been a dream. To ground himself, he closed his eyes.

A bell sounded, and he realized his feet could not feel the floor of the plane and unless he looked down he would not know whether or not his elbows were touching the armrests. But he only gazed straight ahead, his eyes fixing on a flight attendant handing a cup of coffee to a man sitting three rows ahead of him. And as he watched the man, whose face he could not see, grasp the cup, what came to mind was a cold winter morning in a Scranton diner a few years before where he'd overheard two men in the booth behind him talking about someone named Les Wallace. Jacob had been on his way to Cleveland for an early afternoon meeting with a potential client and had stopped in to the diner for a quick breakfast. He was tired and edgy. Because of his late start from New York, he'd driven most of the night and still had five more hours to go. As he sipped his lukewarm coffee, he heard the two men speak about Les, how Wallace had won a tricky case in appeals court, that he was charismatic, neither too old nor too young. Jacob's interest had been piqued. On the back of the receipt from his meal he'd made a note of what he'd heard and put it in his wallet. When he rose to leave, he saw that the men were no longer there; he'd been disappointed.

Three months later he noticed the receipt sticking out of his bill folder and remembered. He was determined to meet Les Wallace: he first called him, introduced himself, asked if he'd ever considered politics, running for a seat in Congress. Then a few weeks later he arranged to meet with Les in Scranton, at his office.

Les, a solemn-looking man, attractive but not in an intimidating way, gently smiled. He reminded Jacob a little of his own father, his overall demeanor, the same kindness and at the same time inscrutableness. As Jacob spoke, Les, sitting behind his desk, looked away, out the large window, seeming to watch the sun set, tapping his forefinger over the top of his shiny desk. Once the sun was no longer visible and the sky had darkened some, shadows crisscrossed the room. It was Jacob's cue to stop talking. Ten minutes later, Les turned to him and said yes, his hazel eyes beginning to light up, but only partially so. And Jacob understood that Les was hesitant—so much like his father, he'd thought.

Although it was Les's first venture into politics, it wasn't Jacob's. And up until then all the candidates he'd worked for had won.

It had been a summer with an insistent sun and he, in the midst of a campaign, had been organizing, managing, and artfully evading intrusive questions from the press about Les. What he had most relished was one late August outdoor rally at a community fair. Les had followed a country music band, well known in the state, at about three in the afternoon.

Les stood on stage, his stance relaxed, dressed in a pale blue short-sleeved shirt, no tie, and off-white chinos. Jacob had gone down into the crowd with a microphone in his hand, sweat pouring down his face, taking questions from the audience. Cool and easy, Les competently answered whatever was asked of him. How thorough he was, Jacob had thought, pleased that he'd found someone like Les.

But once fall set in, Jacob had noticed a change—momentum was shifting. He'd always had good instincts about the ebb and flow of a race, but he wasn't certain what had precipitated this change. He became more anxious, more strident, abrupt with those who were also working on the campaign. He refused to think about the interview on a local television station where he, standing in for Les, had forcefully and indignantly misrepresented the views of the opposing candidate. He hadn't actually lied about her, but had knowingly twisted her words.

He didn't want to acknowledge that underneath he had believed he could fool most of the voters most of the time—people were distracted by the complexities of their own lives, and were easily swayed by generalities, hyperbole.

When his candidate lost by ten percentage points, Jacob wondered if he'd lost his touch as a campaign manager, or if his touch, so to speak, had been an illusion after all. Maybe he'd never had any "touch" at all, he'd simply been lucky, his candidates had been able politicians.

Although Les blamed himself, his political inexperience, Jacob believed Les thought he, Jacob, had been more at fault. He had not positioned Les in the best of lights by arranging morning press interviews for him. For Les, not a morning person, would have appeared more fluid, less hazy, in the afternoon. And then there had been Jacob's own actions. He'd been overly adamant with the local press, and at times nearly angry when defending Les's positions.

In the days following the election, Jacob was stunned, believing he'd never be hired again. At first he blamed Les, thought he was too much like his father—people didn't like candidates who were inscrutable. But underneath he knew Les, though not perfect, was a good man and would have represented his constituents well. For a few days he had toyed with the idea of calling the opposing candidate, congratulating her on her victory, apologizing for not having been completely honest about her record, her policies. But once he put her number in his phone, his heart beat uncontrollably, he felt his face redden, and, when he was told she was in a meeting, his relief was overwhelming. He did not leave his name with her assistant and did not call again. Later he would attribute his not trying a second time to Catherine's accident—naturally he'd been diverted.

In each election a certain truth is revealed. That had been his mistake—when it came to politics he'd always thought truth was irrelevant. He should have known better, Jacob had told himself repeatedly.

One week after the election, he was back in Philadelphia meeting with a colleague, a short, dark-haired man with a slight squint. Over lunch he reassured Jacob that his career was not over, that he knew of a businessman looking to run for the state senate in the next election. Dolefully Jacob had agreed to meet with the candidate.

After the meal, as he stood outside the restaurant, shaking hands and saying good-bye to his colleague, his cell phone rang. When he heard an uncharacteristic strain in his father's voice, he knew something had happened. As he'd just arrived in Philadelphia at eleven o'clock that morning, Jacob had not realized Catherine had come to the city for a visit a few days before. And when he heard his father's grainy voice relay the details of Catherine's car accident, how hopeless her condition was, he felt his life sliding away from him; he needed to hold on to something.

Within thirty minutes he was in his parents' home, running up the stairway and into his old bedroom, not knowing what he was looking for. He opened the closet door, bent down and went through a cardboard box of his old belongings, and soon came across *The Five Chinese Brothers,* a book he'd perused again and again as a child, one he had insisted on reading to Catherine when he'd outgrown it. But she had not liked it intuitively—she had put her small hand over the page, her tiny nails, the red polish on them beginning to chip, as he was reading to her. She looked up at him and said softly, "Jake, I think this is a book for boys, not girls."

He sat stunned on the twin bed, studied the pictures, tracing over them with his long, thick forefinger. When he'd read it as a child, he'd felt reassured—there were such things as miracles. But looking at it again after all these years he understood that between the lines there was a certain dark irony to the story. He got up and flung the book onto the bed. He wanted Catherine conscious again, he kept repeating to himself as he hurried down the stairway and out the door.

A flight attendant now approached him, lowered her head close to his, asked if he'd like some water. She had a round face and a flat smooth forehead, with fine and comforting lines surrounding her eyes. After she handed him a cup, he took a few quick sips, then a deep breath, moving his head slightly to the side. He gripped the plastic cup and closed his eyes, finding it difficult to grasp that he was heading toward Europe. Things had happened so fast over the past two and a half weeks, and he'd been numb the whole time.

His friend Royce was the one who had suggested he go to Paris. He'd found a place for Jacob to stay in a suburb of the city for the month of December—it belonged to a friend of a friend, a foreign correspondent, who was in the Middle East now, writing an article for a Sacramento newspaper. As a local radio talk show host in the Los Angeles area, Royce came in contact with a variety of people.

After a meal that had been efficiently served by the same flight attendant—her lilac-scented perfume had had a soothing effect on him—he fell asleep thinking of Catherine, how she'd look at him, her eyes sparkling even when she was angry or displeased, as if despite it all he was still her hero, and then he thought of her lying in the hospital bed, expressionless.

When he awakened, the plane was filled with light and he heard over the intercom that they'd soon be landing.

From the airport, he took a taxi to the hotel where he'd be staying for one night. The townhouse, about twenty miles southeast of Paris, would not be available until the next day.

Once inside the hotel room, he dropped his suitcase onto the floor, then fell onto the bed. Facedown, he lay there with his clothes on, even his trench coat; on either side of him his large hands were raised, and he clutched the blue and beige comforter as if he were out in the middle of the ocean grasping onto a life raft.

Greta walked with her hands squeezed in the narrow pockets of her green woolen jacket, her chin tucked down as if she were avoiding the wind, but there was no wind in Paris this second day of December, only now and then an emphatic cool breeze. Within she felt the commingling of deep sadness and piercing anxiety. For she was unable to see beyond the present—her future appeared to her as a blank screen, and at this moment she had no desire or foresight to anticipate which images would emerge.

She made her way over one of the footbridges crossing the Seine, then stopped midway and stood close to the railing. She raised her head and gazed out at the expanse of the city, catching sight of the Eiffel Tower at one end and Notre-Dame Cathedral at the other. Like the sky, the river was more gray than blue. The boats motoring up and down the Seine were crowded with tourists, huddled together, many with drinks in hand, craning their necks to view the landmarks they passed.

Although she was in Paris, gazing absently upon its most auspicious sites, she was preoccupied with Florence—she did not know when she'd be able to return to Italy, a thought she found incomprehensible and painful. As she walked along Rue de la Bûcherie, at times she was unaware of her surroundings, expecting to run into her professor or one of her classmates.

And she'd imagine what it would be like if Tommaso was with her, pointing out and commenting on the shape of the Louvre or the architectural style of the Palais du Luxembourg—as much as she tried, she could not shake the memory of his presence. She'd first relish these thoughts of him and then a few minutes later would be shaken by the reality of his absence.

By the time she reached Notre-Dame Cathedral, it had begun to grow dark. Just as she headed toward the main entrance, the lights on the Christmas tree in front of the church flashed on, illuminating the front row of stone figures—sculptures of Israeli kings. Then her gaze fell darkly upon the statues of demonic-looking gargoyles emerging from the sides of the cathedral as if about to leap off, transporting her back to Florence and the mystique of that city, a city that had mesmerized her like no other.

Behind her she heard a group of Italian-speaking tourists. It was startling, similar to recognizing someone from her hometown, the cadence of the Italian language had become that familiar to her. She turned to look at them, a large family, a mother and father perhaps, grandmother, aunt, and three teenage children. She longed to go up to them and converse, tell them how much she had enjoyed living in their country, how kind their people had been to her, how much she missed Italy. But she couldn't because it would have been a sharp reminder of her separation now from Florence and Tommaso.

Again studying the family, she reflexively searched for Tommaso in the group, perhaps in the form of a distant relative who had suddenly shown up to meet them. When they all went into the cathedral without another member having come, she was disappointed.

To distract herself she looked up in the direction of the gargoyles, and her cell phone rang. She dug into her pocketbook, but when she finally pulled it out, it had stopped. The call had come from Italy, but she did not recognize the number.

She turned away from the cathedral and walked hurriedly down Rue Saint-Julien le Pauvre toward her hotel, anxious to know who had attempted to contact her. Her professor should have departed Florence by now, as would have all the members of her class. She deeply regretted having left so quickly. She should have stayed to comprehend what had happened to Tommaso.

Still in her hand, the phone rang again. She froze, dropped it back into her pocketbook, and then stopped walking to catch her breath. The sky had darkened, and she felt more alone than she had ever thought possible. Soon she reached the Latin Quarter; the narrow streets were teeming with people and rife with the smell of sizzling lamb. She went inside a café to order an aperitif. As she sat in the small crowded shop, the hum from various conversations surrounding her, she closed her eyes. Once she and Tommaso had separated from their group outside of the Uffizi that last afternoon in Florence—having agreed to meet the others in a few hours at their favorite restaurant for their final dinner together—she had immediately felt his hand grasping hers. She and Tommaso then strolled toward the Piazza della Signoria. Tommaso was subdued after his performance before the *Venus of Urbino* and uncharacteristically serious. His voice solemn, he said he needed to speak with her before she left Florence, his ring hard against her fingers.

Her heart now pounding, she finished her drink, signaled for the waiter, and paid him, leaving a larger tip than intended. Then she headed in the direction of her hotel. Because of the throngs of people, she had to walk at a slower pace, weaving her way in and out of the crowds. She stopped in front of a store window with a designer shoe collection and stared for a while, not taking in what was before her. When she caught her reflection in the glass, she saw how frightened she looked. And so she walked on.

When she reached the hotel, she was restive, paced in her room for a while, then went back out into the city.

For dinner she walked to Les Deux Magots, a short distance from her hotel. She sat outside, near an aluminum heater, wrapping her jacket close to her form, watching the mist descend as she ate a salad and drank a glass of red wine. Again it was as if Tommaso were at the table with her, smoking, commenting on the history of the café, saying people should go to the restaurant not because of the artists who had frequented it in the past, but because of the present patrons—study each one, he'd say. If you look closely enough perhaps you can determine who may be a budding Picasso or Joyce. That is what he would have said. Yet his lips would have curled into a smile as if he were mocking himself at the same time. If it were afternoon, his head would be tilted back, his eyes on a cloud he found to be an unusual shape. "Look, Greta," he'd call out, pointing it out with his hand, a burning cigarette between his fingers, a beatific expression on his face, "it looks like a rhinoceros. Can you see the horns?"

Finishing her salad and taking a last sip of wine, the liquid warming her throat, she shook away any thoughts of Tommaso. Before leaving the restaurant, she went inside to look at the statues of *les deux magots* themselves, the two figurines from China, not identical at all, only similar in the grace of their poses and the impassive expressions on their faces.

When she left the restaurant, she found a taxi near the subway. When she asked the driver to bring her to the Champs-Élysées, he looked puzzled. Though she had been in Paris for only two days, she was beginning to feel confident experimenting with French words. She knew her pronunciation was not any better but had realized that because she was a stranger to this city, what was most important was to express herself openly and willingly, no matter how poorly. She was beginning to appreciate the subtleties of the French language—you say *blanc* without pronouncing the *c*, but you must imagine the hard *c* sound in order for the listener to comprehend the word.

"Arc de Triomphe?" he asked.

"*Oui*," she said distractedly, her thoughts already beginning to wander back to Tommaso.

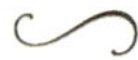

From the Arc de Triomphe and in the glare of the dazzling lights she made her way down the Champs-Élysées—blue, gold, and white bulbs were strung out across the avenue.

She walked past car shops with trendy automobiles parked on the display ramps. Blazing footlights in the front windows of high-fashion clothing stores enhanced the displays of exotically dressed mannequins.

She came upon a small mall; noticing a parfumerie, she went inside. Dazed by the strong lighting, she reached for one sample bottle after another, dabbing perfume from each one behind her ears. Then she went over to an arrangement of lipsticks, more shades than she would have ever thought possible. Holding a tube in her hand, she heard it clink against Tommaso's ring.

Finally she was drawn to the hand creams, the bottles elaborate yet refined. She took off her jacket and placed it on the counter, then she picked up the first container on display and poured some of its contents onto her palm, slowly rubbing it over her hands. The scent of the cream, sweet, sharp, and acrid, reminded her of Tommaso. The more she tried to recall why this was, the more cream she fervently applied, massaging her wrists, her fingers, as if in doing so she was performing a ritual that would in one way or another bring Tommaso to her. Then she closed her eyes, recalling the exotic and seductive smell of the tobacco he smoked.

When Jacob woke, it was pitch dark. He got up from the bed, made his way over to the window, and pulled up the blinds. The street lights glowed in the dark, like a row of brilliant stars hooded by the clouds. Suddenly he was hungry. Still wearing the clothes he'd slept in, he went down to the lobby. Then leaving the hotel, he walked across the quiet street, entering the first restaurant he came upon, small white bulbs framing the two front windows.

After a three-course meal and almost a bottle of a tart red wine, he made his way outside and walked about a quarter of a mile, the night air fresh and cool. He soon noticed a line of taxis in front of an American hotel. He got into one, asking the driver in nearly perfect French to drive to the closest parfumerie. His parents had sent him and Catherine to a French elementary school. He thought of his mother, looking frail, halfheartedly asking him to buy her Parisian perfume when he'd told her he'd be going to France for a month.

When he went inside the parfumerie, he found the lights glaring. Sluggishly he walked by displays of lipsticks, facial moisturizers, and, just before the perfume counter, he saw a variety of hand creams.

Still foggy from the wine, he thought at first he was imagining a woman dressed in a fitted black dress, applying cream to her hands in a rhapsodic, almost trancelike, way. He was not able to take his eyes from her. She was about five foot six, but looked smaller because she was slight. He couldn't tell her age; there was something very young, yet at the same time very mature, about her. Her skin was a slight ruddy color, her hair dark brown with a reddish cast. Gazing at her, he was drawn to the narrow yet curvy slope of her shoulders, the smallness of her waist. In her repetitive movements, he recognized a familiar angst and felt a dryness in his throat. Was she French? He kept his distance, noticed her reflection in the long mirror next to her. As imperfect as the glass was, he found her image as haunting as her actual being. Suddenly she stopped, looked up, now seemingly more aware of her surroundings, her expression quite determined. Swiftly, she put on the jacket that had been lying on the counter. Then, taking long strides, she made her way toward the store exit. Maybe she wasn't French, he thought. No longer sluggish, he followed her. Just as she opened the glass door and passed over the threshold, he saw something fall. But she kept on walking. He went over to the door and saw a gold ring lying there. She must have dropped it. He picked it up; it felt slippery from the cream. It belonged to her, he thought. Gently he tossed the ring up into the air. Catching it, he was momentarily enlivened.

She thrust open the door of the parfumerie and began to walk briskly down the Champs-Élysées. Soon she heard a distinctly American voice—male and sharp—shout out, "Hey there, miss!" The cool night air pressed her face as she turned round. Despite the crowd of people milling along the boulevard, Greta intuitively knew she was the one he wanted. He strode toward her, waving one arm, his beige raincoat unfurling behind him. His build was solid, his gait loose, his ankles slim. Then she lost sight of him. But he was tall and within moments she picked him out again, his head above the crowd. Dark brown hair, a mustache, his expression puzzled, as if trying to remember where he'd seen her before.

He looked disconcerted and hesitant as he approached, she thought. Then she felt his hand lightly touch her shoulder. He lowered his head and didn't speak. With the agility of an illusionist, he opened his other hand; in his palm she saw Tommaso's ring. She checked her forefinger, found it bare, then reflexively snatched the jewelry from him and grasped it tightly, her heart beating wildly.

"It *is* yours," he said, raising his head, his voice deep and clear, as he if were accustomed to speaking in public.

Studying the ring, she thought it appeared smaller; under the bright lights slight scratches were revealed. When she looked back up at him, he said, "Jacob. Jacob Printz."

"You are an American," she said faintly, shaky at the thought of how close she'd come to losing Tommaso's ring.

"You sound disappointed," he said in a murmur.

"That you are an American?" she asked hazily. "I don't know—you've brought me home, it seems."

"But you aren't home—you are in Paris," he said, pointing in the direction of the Arc de Triomphe, standing distant and superior. She looked up at the sky and saw how black it was. Then suddenly it appeared as if all the lights along the boulevard had been turned up a notch.

As she gazed down at Tommaso's ring in the center of her outstretched palm, her heart began again to beat rapidly—for her, it might be all that remained of him.

Stroking her fingers, she said softly, "I put too much cream on my hands."

Two teenage girls brushed past her, and she felt Jacob briefly take her arm. "Let's have a glass of wine," he said, looking away in search of the nearest café, his hands now thrust in the pockets of his raincoat.

Still stunned from the realization she had nearly lost Tommaso's ring, she didn't refuse.

Turning away from the boulevard, they walked down a side street. A few blocks away they came upon a café with a red canvas canopy. There were a few empty seats outside, close to a long aluminum heater, but they decided instead to go inside. As she followed Jacob to a small table in the back, she slipped Tommaso's ring back onto her forefinger.

Jacob took off his raincoat and flipped it over the back of a chair. She noticed that, despite his height, he was agile and easy in his movements.

Soon a waiter, a middle-aged man with long gray sideburns, approached the table. Jacob ordered a bottle of Vouvray, his French sounding even and unhurried. After the server went to fetch the wine, Jacob turned to her and looked suddenly deflated. He clasped his hands together and hunched forward, his gold watch hitting the glass ashtray to his right. His eyes cast down, he extended his forefinger in the direction of Tommaso's ring but didn't speak. When he looked up, he winced, his brown, deep-set eyes watery, and then turned away as if it was too painful to meet her gaze. She drew her hands beneath the table and then onto her lap so that the ring was no longer visible. For some reason it seemed to upset him, she thought.

Where they sat, the lighting was dim, with just one small candle on their table and one on each of the tables surrounding them. But at the front of the café near the windows, customers, talking and gesticulating, were bathed in recessed light from the ceiling.

Jacob was silent and wore an uncertain look, and she noticed one side of his face trembled slightly as if he were about to reveal something of importance, but he did not utter one word. To fill the void she spoke quickly, explaining that she had been in Florence for a three-month art history seminar. Hearing an edginess in her tone, she told him she'd be returning to the United States in ten days or so and was not looking forward to it—she needed to search for a job. Privately she was aware her unease had less to do with finding a job and more to do with leaving Europe, eradicating the very distant possibility of ever seeing Tommaso again.

"Why?" he asked. His searching gaze unsettled her.

"I like Europe better. Italy, I mean. Visually our country seems less vibrant, colorful. When I was young, I'd often look at a magazine photograph of Venice or Rome or Florence—and long to be there."

"Where did you grow up?"

"New England, near Boston," she answered directly, recalling her childhood and the long, slow drives out to Springfield to visit her grandparents. And then she felt a pang, remembering that her grandmother was not well.

"Colorful autumns? Warm summers? Cape Cod? Isn't that what New England is all about?" he asked bemusedly.

"Winter predominates—it stretches from late fall through much of the spring," she countered, feeling assured by the weight of Tommaso's ring on her finger. "The colorful autumns and warm summers are fleeting."

"Perhaps you should return to Italy," he said decidedly.

"One day I will, but first I need to find a job in the United States, most likely in New England."

"Why New England?"

"That is what I know," she said, studying him.

Again he avoided her gaze, told her he'd grown up in Philadelphia. "Winters are long there, too," he added quietly. "One day not too long ago, I came home and realized I no longer belonged there. It felt strange," he said. "The faces of the people on the streets seemed different, less responsive, less interesting. But soon I realized it wasn't them, it was me—I'd lost touch. It's because I travel so much for my work. I'm away much of the time. It caught up with me."

"Have you lost touch with your friends, too?" she asked.

"My friends are scattered now—they live all over the country, the world," he said.

The waiter came with the bottle of Vouvray. Easily opening it, he then poured out the wine. They touched glasses. She kept one hand on her lap.

"To finding your jewelry," Jacob said. For the first time he looked directly at her, and in his gaze she noticed his sadness, shaded with a trace of fear.

"What sort of work do you do that takes you away from home so much—that leaves you friendless?" she asked, bringing the glass to her mouth.

"Politics," he said simply.

Although the dim candlelight cast long shadows, she was able to determine his top lip was more narrow than his bottom one; neither the darkened room nor his slight mustache could hide that.

"Politics?" she echoed. "But what do you do?"

"Promote candidates," he said easily, placing his glass on the table.

For some reason she was disappointed—she had expected more. "Which side are you on?" she asked warily.

"Both," he said.

"Both?"

"Yes, I will promote whoever is willing to pay me."

"Not very ethical, is it?" she asked, feeling disconcerted. Then, embarrassed by the generality she was about to express, she said pointedly, "I don't like politicians."

"On the whole, neither do I," he said assertively, sitting back in his chair. But soon his speech was tempered. "There are a few politicians I do admire," he continued. "It isn't about a party or a cause, it has to do with the person. The worst politicians are the ones who view their ideology as a religion—it makes them too dour and inflexible. But if someone is basically ethical and hardworking he or she will do what is best for society." He had a faraway look in his eyes as if he were trying to remember how to say a certain phrase in a once-familiar foreign language.

As she leaned forward, hoping he'd speak more, she noticed the lights at the front of the café were lowering. Within seconds they had gone out. Except for the wavering candle flames, it was completely dark. At first there was a hush, followed by mumblings. Then someone screamed. Reflexively she stood up, and suddenly felt pressure from Jacob's large warm hand covering hers.

On the floor of the hotel room, lying on his back, Jacob let his eyes linger sleepily on the shadow of a naked, knobby tree branch crossing the ceiling while Greta lay sleeping on the wide, lumpy bed. She was familiar to him and it wasn't because she resembled or even reminded Jacob of his sister Catherine—she was much too direct, forthright. Even in her not telling the story behind the ring, keeping it from his view, she wasn't trying to be subtle or evasive—she simply didn't want him to know. Wasn't that the very reason it had piqued his interest? He was convinced she wasn't calculating, only private.

Greta was smaller than Catherine, and her complexion had more of a ruddy tinge in contrast to his sister's pale coloring. She did not possess Catherine's stubborn wistfulness—in fact she wasn't wistful at all. Despite all this, for some reason he believed Greta held the key, a tiny but intricate one, to Catherine's life, as if somehow it were embedded in one of the crevices of the thick gold ring she wore on her forefinger. She could have been a close friend of Catherine's, the more stable one of the two, adventurous, but not in as indiscriminate and scattered a way as his sister.

Because he had lost all sense of his physical self, he was not attracted to Greta. It was as if every nerve and muscle in his body had been injected with countless shots of Novocain—he had forgotten what desire was. There were moments when he'd try to recall the feeling, but when he was unsuccessful, he would stop pursuing it, let it drift away. Not knowing how long this state would last, he grudgingly accepted it. As he was convinced his sense of pain and longing would be heightened once the numbness faded away, he was concerned about both returning in full force.

He sat up, propped on his elbows, and saw Greta stirring in her sleep, one arm brushing her face, her hand touching the antique-white headboard. She had gone to bed fully dressed. The jacket she had tossed over the arm of the chair had slipped to the floor.

The previous night they had gone back to his hotel; it was closer to the café than hers. The woman's scream had aborted an attack at the café. Instead of dropping the backpack with the bomb, the culprit had run off—a primitive response, Jacob thought—then he'd been blown up on a side street. No one else had been hurt. The perpetrator must have been young and inexperienced, perhaps even acting on his own. But you never knew for sure. He was amazed at the invincibility of the

French, their strength, their certainty, carrying on business as usual, as if there was a security in their way of life that never truly could be infringed upon. But he believed there was no such thing as certainty, and the only kind he now experienced was in Greta's even breaths as she lay sleeping on the bed in his hotel room.

Lying back down, he attempted to use cold logic to reconstruct the details of the previous evening, as if in doing so he would be allaying his fears and dampening the images intermittently crossing his mind of what *might* have happened. As much as he tried, he could not remember what he and Greta had been discussing, but he vividly recalled how she had leaned forward to listen to him, then a moment later she had abruptly put her glass down on the table and sat back, her shoulders hunched as she looked toward the front of the café. Tracing her gaze, he saw the lights at the front dim and quickly go out. A horrific scream followed within seconds. When Greta stood up, he'd grasped her hand. Loud murmurings. Footsteps. In the darkness, the eight or ten people sitting close to their table had begun to move hurriedly toward the exit. He and Greta followed.

When they reached the street, the police had arrived. A woman about his age, blond hair, dressed in black pants and a red leather jacket, was speaking to the officers, pointing down the street, her French so rapid Jacob could not comprehend her words.

He then spotted the waiter who had served them; his shirtsleeves were now rolled up. He looked up and down the street, an expression of annoyance crossing his face, as if he was waiting for a ride and the driver was late. Approaching him, Jacob, in his careful French, asked what happened.

The waiter stared hard at Jacob, then answered in English, telling them that a man with a backpack had come into the café. That woman, he continued, pointing to the lady speaking to the policemen, was a frequent customer and familiar with the layout of the café. She had noticed the perpetrator stealing behind the bar. When the lights began to lower, she realized he was the one who most likely had turned down the switches. As the waiter spoke, they heard a blast in the distance.

Now as Jacob lay on the hotel room floor, he felt he could not bear any more shocks. The shock of the lost election was the most mild of them all, the worst had been Catherine's death, and this incident was somewhere in the middle. They had not been harmed—he should be grateful, he thought. But he didn't feel that way. Instead he was rattled to the core.

Before going up to his room the previous night, he and Greta had had a drink at the hotel bar. When he caught his reflection in the mirror on the wall, he nearly didn't recognize himself, his head cast downward, his complexion pale. Then out of the corner of his eye, he noticed Greta clutching the gold ring, pressing it with her fingers, as if she were deriving a sense of solidity from it.

He lifted the glass of whiskey to his lips and his hand shook. Then, looking over at Greta, he thought she did not appear tired but intent and in a way becalmed, the fine streaks of gold in her brown eyes giving her an almost exotic appearance.

"These past few days have been like a dream—so unreal," she said so softly it took a few seconds for him to decipher her words. Then she gazed down at the ring and a look of strain crossed her face.

"It does happen," he said, wryly. Sharply she looked up at him.

"But you do not know what I mean," she retorted. And he felt her independence. It was as if she had forgotten about the scare. She looked over at her jacket, lying on the empty stool next to her, as if she was considering leaving and going back to her hotel, but then he saw her eyes widen as if suddenly she was struck by what had happened at the café, as if images of the event were flashing through her mind.

"It's two a.m. We should try to sleep; we may be questioned tomorrow. We gave our names, showed our passports—that may be sufficient. The authorities can easily check into things nowadays," he said.

She nodded and yawned. As he followed her toward the elevator, he studied her erect posture, her narrow shoulders, the light from the chandelier bringing out the red highlights in her brown hair, and it struck him how much of a stranger she was to him—maybe she wasn't simply a young American abroad, mulling over a just-ended affair with a disarming Italian, during a post-college semester abroad, as he had originally guessed. Maybe the ring didn't belong to her. Maybe she had stolen it.

When they got to the room, she turned to him and said, "I trust you because you are from close to home, from Philadelphia—but I don't *know* you."

"We are Americans in a foreign country, who just experienced a terrible scare," he said, trying to sound matter-of-fact, but he heard the tension in his voice.

"Though I've not been here before, at least until this week, I never thought of Paris as part of a foreign country—more a city of the world," she said with a smile, ignoring his words about the scare. Her eyelids began to lower. She tossed her jacket over the arm of the chair and fell onto the bed. Standing over her, he watched until she fell asleep, thinking that maybe what he'd been searching for all along had had nothing to do with an event or a philosophy but with a person, with people. Though soon his mind was empty, and he felt nothing. For as the shock of the near attack at the café was slowly subsiding, his agitation peeling away, his body had begun to numb up again.

Now a faint light trickled into the room. He checked his watch. It was about twenty past six—the sun would not rise for a while. Sitting up, he looked over at the bed; Greta was quite still. He wanted to go to her to see if she was breathing, be reassured she was alive. But soon he saw the gentle rise and fall of her chest. He slumped back down on the floor, closed his eyes, and slept more deeply than he had since he'd left Philadelphia less than thirty hours before.

Over breakfast, he told her he had checked in with the police and that they had been cleared. They sat near a large window; the sun was stronger than yesterday. Between sips of coffee he explained he would be staying about twenty miles southeast of the city, in an apartment of a friend of a friend, a foreign correspondent working somewhere in the Middle East that month.

She nodded and reached for another croissant, the gold ring, loose on her forefinger, picking up the morning light. "Thanks for letting me stay with you and sleep in your bed. You must be exhausted from lying on the floor all night. Maybe you can get some rest before you check out."

"Will you go back to your hotel?" he asked.

"Yes, I will." She sounded resolved, he thought, believing there was something fearless about her.

Then she excused herself and went to the restroom, leaving her phone on the table. He drew out his cell and began to look for any news articles in American papers on what had happened the previous night. Eventually he found one, a short piece, mentioning that no one had been hurt except the perpetrator, that a nearby pastry shop had been badly damaged, and that the person had apparently acted alone.

As he put his cell back in his pocket, he heard a ring. Checking his phone, he realized the sound wasn't coming from his cell, but from Greta's.

Reaching across the table, he picked up her phone and saw the call was from Italy. He put it back down next to her sunglasses and looked in the direction of the restroom. There was no sign of her.

When the phone stopped ringing, he took another sip of coffee. He placed the cup back in the saucer, and the ringing started again. Picking up her cell, he saw the call again was from Italy, and it appeared to be the same number that had been displayed a few moments before. He looked at the time on his watch, realizing he'd have to check out in an hour—that wouldn't leave him much time to rest. And with that thought, he felt defiant—she had robbed him of his bed. Willfully he answered her cell, speaking brusquely, "Good morning, I am answering the phone for Greta Hatler." He'd seen her full name on her passport.

There was silence and then a voice came in, male, sounding frail and a little surprised.

"You speak English only?" he asked.

"Yes," Jacob said firmly.

"I am calling the phone of Greta Hatler?" he asked, his voice sounding clearer but just as weak.

"Yes."

"Please tell her Tommaso Rigoletti is calling."

"Tommaso Rigoletti," Jacob repeated slowly and steadily. But before he'd finished saying the name, Tommaso Rigoletti, whoever that was, the connection had been broken.

He turned and saw Greta coming toward him. When he handed her the phone, she looked surprised, her lips slightly opening, a faint reddening of her cheeks. Having brushed her hair back off her face, she now looked smaller, younger. She dropped her phone on the table, then stood behind her chair, as if waiting for an explanation.

"Your phone rang a few times, and stopped. Then it rang again a minute or so later. I picked it up, said I was answering the phone for Greta Hatler."

"My mother?" she asked. Her mouth tensed as she spoke.

"No—it was a man's voice—distant-sounding or weakened."

"Was the call from the United States?" She seemed more anxious now. Nervously she touched her hair, then raised her chin as if to brace herself.

"No, it was from Italy."

"Italy?" she said and leaned forward. Pointedly she asked, "Did he speak in Italian?"

"No, but I believe he would have. I made it clear I did not know Italian, so he spoke in English."

"Did he leave his name? Where he was calling from?" she asked in a worried voice, looking down at the ring on her forefinger.

"Yes, yes, he left his name, but nothing else," he answered, feeling uneasy, wishing he had not picked up the phone.

"What was it?"

"I hope I can pronounce it correctly," he said, hearing an edge in his voice.

"Try," she said insistently, eyeing him more intently, as if she were challenging him in some way.

He paused and said, "Tommaso. Tommaso Rigoletto, or Rigoletti, almost like the opera."

And as he spoke, she turned pale, and grasped the back of her chair to steady herself.

"Sit down," he said. "Please sit down." And he was surprised at how easily she followed his instruction.

Once Jacob had said Tommaso's name, vivid images filled her mind—walking across the Ponte Vecchio with Tommaso, the wind blowing in their faces, the pungent smell of his tobacco, how he'd wind his finger round a strand of her hair, his face close to hers, his eyes glaringly honest whenever he would mention how frustrated he was by what he called the opaqueness of life.

For various reasons she had believed Tommaso would not try and contact her—he might not be alive or could have been seriously injured or he was angry with her for having left Florence so abruptly—at the same time she had expected him to show up in Paris, in the lobby of the hotel, his hand over his heart, asking in a mildly hurt tone, "Why did you not say good-bye, Greta?"

After the initial shock of Tommaso's call had passed, she was relieved to know he was alive, that the accident hadn't been fatal, and then buoyed at the thought that she might see him again. Yet she was in no rush to return his call—it hadn't been his cell number and she needed time. She didn't know what she would say, how she would explain her actions—he most certainly would want to know why she had left so precipitously. And so when Jacob offhandedly had asked if she would be interested in seeing the townhouse he would be staying in, she had readily agreed. It was her way of stalling, postponing the call to Tommaso.

Although she and Jacob each had been traveling alone, their being together now had a natural flow to it, not awkward or pushed or overtly needy. And the incident in the café had bonded them in a way, she thought—as if they secretly believed when they separated the memory of it would be more harsh, or worse, the experience would seem unreal and in a sense would revert to a dream, a dream that would most likely haunt each of them for a long while.

During the forty-minute train ride to the townhouse and through the many abrupt stops, Jacob, his head bowed, his body shaking some from the vibration of the train, read the *New York Times* and *Wall Street Journal* from his phone as he said he would when she'd told him she needed to rest. Tightly closing her eyes, she attempted to recall in detail her last evening with Tommaso.

As they'd strolled across the Piazza della Signoria, Tommaso had spoken adamantly about wanting to live in the United States. He grasped her hand, then suddenly dropped it, put his own to his heart to show how bereft he'd be if he could not realize this dream of his. He held her hand again and as they began to walk, veering away from the center of the square, he spoke about photos he had seen of the Statue of Liberty, the Golden Gate Bridge, and the Liberty Bell, his expression tender. "That crack in the bell," he said, drawing it in the air. At first she was drawn in by his descriptions—it was as if he were introducing her to her country—but she wondered if he would be the same person in the United States; his country, his culture were as much a part of him as his cajoling expression, quixotic humor, and fixed nature.

"But what would you do there?"

"Same as here," he said, surprised by her question.

"Museum work?" she asked, feeling her face redden. To distract herself from the conversation she looked up at the slowly darkening sky. The weather had become much cooler. She shivered. He put his arm around her and said, "Let's go someplace warm." He led her through the narrow, bustling streets toward where he lived. She had gone there with him only once before; he had needed to pick up a book for his talk one afternoon on della Robbia's terra-cotta roundels. Their stay had been brief—she had waited in the doorway—as soon afterward they'd met the others in the group at the Museo degli Innocenti.

They crossed the Ponte Vecchio, their heads down to buttress themselves against the brisk wind coming in from the north, their hands thrust in the pockets of their jackets.

Ten minutes later they came to a four-story brick building. Tommaso and his mother lived on the first floor. She was visiting her sister in Torino, he said, opening the door with a long black key. They walked into a short hallway where a narrow red rug with embossed black diamonds lay on the floor. Taking two steps down, they were in the living area, with the kitchen to the right. Hardwood floors, a black leather sofa, and a dark oak hutch with crystal glasses and bottles of wine, whiskey, and sherry. There were no drapes covering the windows; the apartment faced a school yard that looked desolate now, for there were no leaves on the trees and the children had left for the day.

As Tommaso poured out the sherry, she studied his reflection in the mirror. There was a bemused quality about him, a slight cynicism she had not before noticed—it was in how he moved his mouth to the side. She went over to the window and rested her forehead against the pane, imagining him as a young child walking up the stone steps of the school, his head held high, his eyes alert. He must have been precocious in the classroom, the first to raise his hand in response to a question, waving it in the teacher's face, ready to cry out the answer. She pictured him as rambunctious on the playground, needing to be the leader in whatever game his classmates chose to play—not very tall, he would have been more aggressive than the others, he would play harder with more passion emanating from his blue-green eyes.

She felt him behind her and turned round. Handing her a glass, he took her by the hand, drew her away from the window. "It's dreary outdoors, not a pleasant sight," he said in a gentle, admonishing voice. "I prefer spring."

"I can see you as a child, Tommaso, on that playground."

"What do you imagine?" he asked indifferently, lighting a cigarette as she sat down on the sofa and sipped from her glass.

Resting her head back against the cushion, she closed her eyes, told him her thoughts, and, when she finished speaking and opened them, he was standing before her, his knees touching hers.

His smile was uncharacteristically sheepish; his leonine eyebrows knitting together, his head lowered. "You have it wrong, Greta," he said, his tone deepening. He moved away from her. "I was shy, my father died before I knew him. I had no brothers, no sisters. I was alone. My mother should have had a daughter—she liked looking at clothing for girls, never felt comfortable choosing a present for me. She would often ask her brother to come along to help. My uncle was a nice man, but quiet, thoughtful. He never married, worked in a bank, dreamed of becoming a sculptor, had a studio in the shed close to his home, brought me to museums. That is why I do what I do now. No, Greta, I was not a precocious child."

She thought how sad he must have been as a child, yet at the same time filled with a desire to be more.

"What about your childhood, Greta?" he asked.

Not anticipating his question, she was startled. "I don't know what to say, Tommaso," she responded without thinking. "Nothing ever happened. My parents are and have always been subdued, confined, without hope or desire."

"Oh, Greta," Tommaso had said with a smile, "and so in spirit perhaps our childhoods were not so different then. But still I believe you were the more precocious one; you were the one who was not shy."

At that thought, she felt Jacob nudge her arm. "We will be getting off at the next stop, Greta," he said, his voice sleepy.

She opened her eyes and looked out the window at a gray and empty station, the train not stopping, just passing through. And she felt resentful. She had not wanted to be interrupted from thinking about Tommaso. But when she turned to Jacob, she saw how tired he was, his eyes bloodshot, and she remembered how he had let her sleep in his bed the previous night and now needed to rest. There was more stubble on his chin; he had not had a chance to use the shower or shave.

"I'm ready," she said, looking directly at him, his weary gaze. He was so tired he was not able to respond with anything other than a blank stare as if he were sleeping with his eyes open.

They bought a loaf of fresh French bread from the bakery at the train station and then took a taxi to the townhouse. As they passed rows of naked trees and brown patches of land, she mused over when she should return Tommaso's call. She looked down at the ring covering much of her forefinger and felt a pang.

When she had arrived in Paris she had expected to be contacted by the Florentine police or a member of Tommaso's family who had found her number in his cell.

The taxi stopped before a yellow townhouse. There were five or six other duplicate homes in the lot. Jacob paid the driver and took his suitcase from the trunk. She still had her belongings at the hotel and wasn't certain if she wanted to stay with him. She needed to first understand what he wanted from her, if anything, more than companionship. He was disillusioned and sad, but she trusted him.

The townhouse was spacious, with two floors; the first included a sitting area with French doors that looked out on a small duck pond. A sofa faced the doors, and on the coffee table were *National Geographic* magazines as well as journals with foreign titles she could not decipher.

Jacob went up the stairs and she wandered into the kitchen, trying to adjust herself to her new surroundings. After a while, she went over to the French doors to look out at the ducks. It was late afternoon and no longer sunny; the sky was now gray and hazy. From upstairs she heard Jacob's footsteps and the sound of a shower running. But after a while there was silence and she assumed he had fallen asleep.

As she watched the ducks moving to and fro across the brackish waters, she tried to muster up courage to return Tommaso's call. It had not come from his cell—that number was in her phone. Her heart beating fiercely, she first tried his cell, but it went directly to his voicemail. It was not him speaking, but an automated response from an operator, repeating the full number in a slow and dignified Italian. Immediately Greta clicked off, not wanting to leave a message.

She checked her phone for the most recent call, the one Jacob had said was from Tommaso, noting the number was identical to the one that had come in during her second full day in Paris. She pressed the number, her finger trembling. On the second ring, a woman's voice answered.

"Yes, who is calling?" she asked impatiently.

Greta explained, though her Italian was slow, already rusty.

The woman sounded surprised, perhaps not certain who Tommaso was, but then suddenly, in a decisive voice, she said, "He is no longer here."

"Is he well?" she asked anxiously, her heart beating quickly.

"Are you a family member?" she demanded, her voice suspicious. And she realized she had most likely called a hospital and the woman possibly was a nurse.

"Is he alive?" Greta cried out, her voice shaky, tears springing to her eyes.

"Transferred," she said. "He's been transferred."

Greta believed he would call again. He did not have his cell phone with him, she assumed. He must have memorized her number. And she was hopeful as tears streamed down her face, recalling again how he had insisted he'd been more shy than she as a child. "Maybe you are right, Tommaso—maybe I was the more precocious one," she had answered doubtfully. Smiling, he reached for her hands, pulling her to her feet, the room mostly dark.

Now she heard Jacob's footsteps descending the stairs, calling out her name, apologizing for having fallen asleep, his voice crashing into her thoughts like a cold wave hitting the shore. He told her they would be able to walk into town where they'd have dinner, and then he would rent a car and drive her back to Paris.

But when she turned to him, he caught her gaze and said bluntly, "You've been crying. What's happened?" She saw the shadows beneath his eyes.

"Just tired," she said curtly. She turned away, looked out the French doors, and saw the sun behind gray clouds was about to set, heavy shadows crossing the sitting area, the coffee table, the magazines strewn about.

He came up behind her and said, "I'm sorry, Greta."

"No, don't be sorry. I am the one who took your bed last night—it's been trying these last few days, the scene in the café . . ."

"The call from your Italian friend," he said, looking directly at her.

"I think I should go back to Paris as soon as possible," she said firmly, crossing her arms, walking past him.

"I'd like to help your friend, Greta," he said beseechingly.

"I do not think you can help. You are not a doctor, you cannot heal him."

"What happened to him?"

"Tommaso?" she asked, his name naturally coming from her lips.

"Yes, Tommaso," he responded, lifting his eyebrows, gently mimicking her Italian inflection.

He took her hand—it felt soft and cold; sensing her resistance, he let it go. Looking out the French doors, he watched the steady movement of the ducks gliding across the pond, the sky a heavy gray now, absent any streak of light. Then he turned to meet her gaze; it was neither harsh nor benign, but unflinchingly open.

Although Greta said there was nothing he could do, Jacob believed in some way she was relying on him to help her—that was why she had agreed to come with him. What she hadn't realized was his need for her was greater than hers for him. If she was at all aware of this, he believed it was in a hazy and ungraspable way. Wasn't her mind focused on other things—namely Tommaso and returning home?

"Maybe I can help," he said, glancing at her. "Maybe there is something I can do for your friend that hasn't crossed your mind. But in order to help I first need to know what happened. Who is Tommaso?"

As she moved away from him, he immediately regretted how he had said Tommaso's name. His tone had been accusatory, infused with a subtle anger. Or was he jealous?

The sky had suddenly darkened; he could no longer clearly see the duck pond. He switched on the lamp that stood on the small teakwood table next to the sofa, the light from it spotting a framed copy of a de Kooning painting hanging on the wall. Wasn't the original at the Philadelphia Museum? He hadn't noticed the copy earlier and at first glance thought there was a resemblance, though vague, between Greta and the face of the woman in the painting. He recalled Royce telling him that the journalist whose apartment he'd be staying in, though having worked in Sacramento for five years, had lived most of his life in Philadelphia.

Had he seen the painting at the museum with Catherine? Had she disliked it? Jacob couldn't remember—it was too long ago.

When he turned again to Greta, he saw there were tears running down her long, oval face to the rim of her closed lips, set as if she were a young adolescent refusing to open them, not wanting to reveal the whereabouts of a friend who had run away from home. But her bearing was strong, her pain adult and complicated. And as she sat in silence, her head resting back against the sofa cushion, he imagined what Tommaso must be like—tall, dark haired, a quick wit, an easy walk, tanned, often reaching out to touch her arm or to rest his hand on her shoulder. Though he'd spoken to him that morning, he couldn't remember the sound of Tommaso's voice. Their short phone exchange may as well have happened a week before; the tenor of Tommaso's speech had already faded from memory.

Again he looked at the copy of the de Kooning, deciding it didn't resemble Greta at all. It had been wishful thinking on his part; he had wanted to view her as someone distant, existing within a certain framework, untouchable and unreachable. But sitting next to him, she was real, breathing deeply, her chest rising and falling. A shadow sliced her form in two; facing him was the darker side.

Intently he studied her closed eyes, her eyelids soft and spongy, her arms languorously resting on either side of her, her hands open, revealing her naked white palms. Gazing at her crossed legs in sheer black stockings, he noticed a birthmark on the inner part of her right ankle, round and red like a bee sting. In a sense she had been stung, he thought, but by whom—Tommaso, or was it someone else?

Instinctively he believed Greta in some way would soon shed light on his sister's short existence, and because of this her presence distracted him from darker thoughts and more painful memories of Catherine.

It wasn't because he was traveling solo that he needed her—he'd done that for years; it was natural for him—but it was because now he was alone with this new life of his, the one that had emerged in the aftermath of Catherine's death. He was convinced Greta would be able to help him fill the void between what he had been and what he was becoming.

She was young, he thought, yet in another way old—he had realized this about her when he had first noticed her, how she had applied the cream so ardently over her long, agile hands. She had known pain, disappointment.

Her eyes shut, she spoke softly. He leaned closer to her, his ear nearly brushing hers.

"I think he's dying," she said quietly. "I know it, I feel it."

He wanted to refute her words, but he believed if he did so she would cease speaking.

Without opening her eyes, she raised her hand, fingers down, swaying it back and forth, like a pendulum; she did so until the ring fell from her finger and onto the braided rug near her feet.

"I do not want to carry the illusion of him any longer," she said, as if she were making a wish.

"I spoke with him this morning. He is not dead. I am certain of it," he said, sounding for a moment, he thought, like the old Jake Printz, his voice calm, persistent, and subtly false.

When he finished, she opened her eyes and rolled her head toward him. "You aren't convincing," she said and despite her sadness, she faintly smiled.

"I never really was," he said wryly, and the old Jacob vanished as if he'd never been.

He got up and went into the small kitchen, rummaging about; it was too small a space for him but the ceiling was high. Bending his head not out of necessity but habit, he opened and shut doors until he found two unopened bottles of wine tucked away in the back of the top right cabinet. Holding one of the bottles in his hand, he took note of the year and name so he could replace it. Then he looked around for an opener and soon found it lying on the black granite counter next to the coffee maker, a few inches from the sink.

Intending to give her a sense of privacy, he refrained from glancing into the living area and kept the kitchen lights dim. After pouring out two glasses of the red velvety liquid, he carried them into the room and found her lying curled on the sofa. When he saw she was asleep, he put her glass on the end table and sat in the armchair across from her.

He wondered what she was dreaming of—the scare they'd had the previous evening at the café? Tommaso? Studying her, her hand dangling, her head tucked inside the bend in her arm, her knees raised almost to her chest, he had a fleeting image of Catherine at nine or so, running into their home, her cheeks flushed from excitement, announcing that she had been invited to the birthday party of the most well-liked girl in her class. She jumped up and down, then ran toward the kitchen, sliding on the recently polished hardwood floor, falling into the position Greta now lay. His gaze caressing her sleeping form, he wondered if in his old life he would have been attracted to Greta.

He had not been involved with too many women over the years—three, maybe four. His relationships had been lively, tongue-in-cheek, to an extent. Humor had been his mainstay—some had even fallen in love with him because of it.

During the course of a relationship he would cherish the name of a woman, often repeating it when he was in her presence or with a friend. Gregarious and enthusiastic about trying different things, he had even attempted skydiving once, with Jenna, who'd had her pilot's license. The breakups had been mostly mutual, nearly always ending on a poignant yet upbeat note. But one of his relationships had not been that way. She was a pianist. Her name was Alene. He'd met her at a cocktail party in Philadelphia; she was a friend of a friend's wife. Soon after they'd been introduced, they were talking alone and she had asked him why he had chosen a career in politics. When he told her what he had not revealed to anyone else, that he had done so because he'd been influenced by the writings of John Locke, she had been intrigued. Artistic women had never really taken to him before and he had been flattered, then curious.

Whenever he attended one of Alene's concerts he became restless. Classical music had never interested him. What he liked was not what she played but how she played, the movement of her shoulders, her arms extending in a firm, passionate way, her fingers long and emphatic, and how in the concert hall the lights shone down on her, on her long, black dress. He'd found Alene haunting—it had been a new experience for him.

But she grew weary of him, finding him emotionally hollow in his need to use humor regardless of the circumstance, as if it were a cure of some sort; no, they were not compatible, she had said, her eyes small, green, and penetrating. For a while afterward, he'd shudder at the thought of her.

But now, looking at Greta lying on the sofa, he wondered if Alene had been right—there was something vacuous about his temperament—he wasn't real. Perhaps over the years he'd become a deficient copy of his true self, whomever that may be. He felt a stab of remorse. Catherine, he thought, needing her to be with him now, longing to tease her as he had done even when they were older. For in chiding the twenty-or-so-year-old Catherine he had believed he was protecting her as he had when she was young and unknowing. He had never acted ineptly in her presence because she had made him feel whole, his life worthwhile.

He noticed Greta's head moving, the silky strands of her hair clinging together.

"Jacob?" she called out.

"I'm here," he said softly, affirmatively.

Sitting up, she turned toward him. "Sorry, I must have dozed off," she said, her voice groggy from sleep. Her eyes fixed on the glass of wine on the table. "For me?" she asked, sounding more awake.

He nodded and she reached for the glass, cupping it in her hands, looking over at him, her eyes bleary. Then she tossed back her head, brought the wine to her lips, and dispassionately he watched the liquid make its way down her slender throat.

After a few slow sips, she put the glass back on the table.

He caught her gaze. "Who is Tommaso?" he asked, hearing a parental sternness in his voice.

The dim light from the lamp caressed her narrow cheekbones: "You mean, who *was* Tommaso," she said.

She sounded resigned and he was surprised. "You do not know that he is not alive just as I do not know for certain that he is," he answered, sounding both solemn and slightly exasperated.

When she looked over at him, her expression was pained. "I believe he called this morning to say good-bye to me."

At her words, Jacob felt a sense of panic and slowly sat back in his chair, his shoulders hunched, as if shrugging off the last remnants of his former self.

She thought he appeared lost, sitting in the chair with his hands grasping his knees, wearing a dazed expression, his slightly opened legs revealing a steady masculinity, mature but not yet ripened.

For a moment she forgot about Tommaso. But she was no longer able to see Jacob clearly; he was masked by a shadow. Had he shifted in his chair? When he spoke, his voice was soft and direct, different from before—as if he had thought about his words prior to talking instead of spewing out what he believed was most convenient. "You don't know if what you are saying is true. You may be imagining his death because you are no longer with him, because you have parted from him."

An outside light above the French doors went on, illuminating Jacob's expression, and she could see him lift his gaze to the copy of the de Kooning on the wall, his nose long and narrow, sharp, his small, close-set, dark eyes studying the work as if he were gleaning some sort of knowledge from it.

Her heart beat swiftly; she felt caught. The light went off and she looked past the French doors, out into the still evening. She forced herself to speak and although she made an effort to control it, she thought her voice sounded shaky. "Tommaso Rigoletti was an assistant lecturer—I guess you could say. Our professor, Beth Rogers, met him in Florence on a cold, rainy spring afternoon, at the Florence Baptistery, in front of Ghiberti's bronze doors. He was leading a tour of both Americans and Sicilians and Beth was there alone on her school holiday break. She listened in as if she were part of his tour group, and was impressed with Tommaso's knowledge of art. Not only was Tommaso charismatic, Beth had said to us, but he engaged his audience—they became part of the discussion, and so in a sense part of the art. After the group dispersed for lunch, she went up to him, introduced herself, and said how much she had enjoyed his lecture. She told him his talk had given her an idea. Could they discuss it over dinner that evening—her treat?

"According to Beth—she told us all this one night at our last group get-together before we left for Florence—their first dinner together lasted four hours. They dined at a restaurant only the locals and foreigners familiar with Florence knew of. But that evening they did not speak about their mutual love of paintings, sculptures, or even Ghiberti's bronze doors—instead they spoke about what they each most desired. Beth never said how the topic came up, but after a few glasses of wine they were, to say the least, at ease with each other. She never told us what it was they each most desired, but she did say they also had discussed their favorite movies—both preferred older films; hers was *Cinema Paradiso,* and his was *Raging Bull.* And that had been the point when they'd bonded, for she liked an Italian film, and he preferred an American director—it was, she said, like crossing arms and drinking wine from each other's glass. At the end of their meal, she asked him to be part of our group. He was hesitant at first, said he was accustomed to leading tours that were more international in makeup. Part of the challenge for him was to bring different cultures together to see if his presentation was viable for all. And during a discussion he liked switching, for example, from Italian to English. He spoke five languages. Although Beth's appearance was somewhat scattered, her blouse never completely tucked in her skirt or pants, her fine hair rarely in place, the belt of her raincoat always loose, her opinions were determined and persuasive. And so eventually Tommaso agreed to be part of our group. That was a year and a half before our semester in Florence."

She looked over at Jacob. He was leaning forward in the chair, his eyes closed, listening intently to her words. After taking a deep breath, she continued, her voice no longer shaky, she thought, but matter-of-fact.

"Almost from the start Tommaso was adored by all the women in our group—but in different ways. It was obvious he and Beth had established a strong friendship. She had visited Florence several times since meeting him. There was a seven-year age difference between the two of them—she was older than Tommaso. I didn't know if their relationship was solely professional. In college there had been talk about Beth with another male professor, married, I think, and maybe a graduate student as well. I never paid much attention to those rumors. It was purposeful on my part. I didn't want to know. Occasionally she'd look at Tommaso endearingly but at other times she'd seem at a distance from him, especially when they discussed particular works of art. I wanted to believe their relationship was platonic. One day we climbed to the top of the Duomo, and on the way down we were in close proximity to the paintings Vasari had begun. And as we made our way farther down, Beth and Tommaso began an intense discussion about the significance of Vasari's work. But it was heated in an intellectual way, more than in an emotional one."

Greta stopped speaking; she felt exposed, and uncertain whether or not Jacob wanted to hear more. But soon he said, "Please, Greta, go on. I'm hooked. "

She was surprised; she couldn't imagine what had hooked him. But as she noted his steady, concentrated expression she wondered if for some unknown reason he had been "hooked," so to speak, before she had even begun.

"Others liked Tommaso as well," she continued evenly, "but, as I said, in different ways. Most liked him because he was creative, erudite, and had a compelling sense of humor. He could make us laugh even if we were tired and serious. But despite his insistence on speaking with us only in English, some of the women also found him to be foreign, too much so for their tastes. They savored his personality, nothing more. Then there were the three of us: Elaine, Patty, and myself. We were all curious about him, and so became more and more attracted to him. Naturally, we were all aware of one another's attraction and would silently gauge the effect each of us had on him. And because of this, we were drawn together. One night, we had been in Florence for about two weeks and were returning from a party given by American students from another college spending a semester in the city. Walking back to the dormitory, we were a little woozy from having had too much to drink, so we linked arms to keep our balance. Because of the full moon, it was not too dark. Patty and I began to emphatically discuss Tommaso, our voices louder than usual, both deciding that he must be most attracted to Elaine. It was simple, we said. She was small, but not slim, long dark hair, dark eyes, and a seductive smile. Patricia and I decided Tommaso and Elaine would look good together as a couple, suit each other physically."

Greta stopped talking and watched Jacob as he got up and came to sit next to her. He picked up Tommaso's ring from the floor, studied it for a while, then turned to her and said, "Go on."

She took another sip of wine, and continued. "But those early few days when I first met Tommaso, my impression of him was not a favorable one. I didn't like him at all, thought he was not very real—I found him to be a character of sorts. He dressed as if he were about to be photographed for a fashion magazine. He was not very tall—we may have been the same height, or maybe he was a few inches taller than me. But his fascinating personality made him seem taller than he was, I think. And so, his interest in clothes, his larger-than-life personality at first put me at a distance from him. Though I did believe he was very knowledgeable about art."

"But a week or two later you liked him very much, you changed toward him, your feelings, impressions?" Jacob sounded quiet, but earnest.

Out of the corner of her eye, she saw he was looking at her, not at the ring, which he held loosely in the palm of his left hand.

"Yes, I did change because I began to believe he was genuine, he was real."

"And you were the one he liked best, not Elaine," Jacob said.

"Oh, I don't know—Tommaso never did choose favorites, he was quite professional that way—he didn't prefer one student over another, it wasn't in his nature to do so. He liked people equally."

"But this is his ring, isn't it? And you are the one who has it," Jacob said softly, thoughtfully, looking down at the ring in the palm of his hand. Then, raising his head, he continued in the same tone. "He gave it to you, unless you stole it. But you are not a thief, are you?" And he caught her gaze.

"Of course I am not a thief," she answered hastily. "Yes, it is Tommaso's ring, and no, I did not take it from him."

Her heart began to beat quickly. Again, she felt caught—she knew she had the ring because Tommaso must have given it to her, but she could not remember the circumstances.

She stood up and walked to the French doors. "We did not become involved until the last two weeks of our stay, and then when we were about to part—I'd be taking the train to Paris the next day and needed to finish packing—the accident happened. He was hit by a car. It was dark, he was wearing black. I cannot remember much about it. All I recall is leaving early the next day, not knowing if he would be okay."

Because the inside light was on, she could not look out past the French doors, but instead was faced with her own wavering reflection in the glass. She turned and saw Jacob sitting erectly, an expression of earnest curiosity crossing his face. She met his gaze. "Why did I run away?" she asked aloud, hearing the angst in her voice. Overcome by a sense of loss, she moved toward Jacob; as she held out her hand to him, there was a knock at the door.

Jacob went to the door and opened it, but no one was there. A strong gust of wind swept by; he shivered, and for a moment he envisioned his friend Royce standing on the threshold with an insistent smile crossing his fleshy lips. Jacob looked up at the darkening sky and saw snow slowly begin to fall, in thick clusters, like matted cotton, and he quickly shut the door.

Greta had come in to the foyer, loosely holding the wine glass in her raised hand. He thought she looked pale. "It must have been the wind," he said bluntly, hearing a thread of disappointment in his voice.

"The wind," she repeated.

"It's started to snow—maybe we should have dinner here."

While they rummaged through the kitchen in search of food to eat along with the loaf of bread they had bought at the train station, he thought again of his friend and was pained. It struck him that only three months before he had been with Royce and Catherine at the bar in downtown

Philadelphia—it was as if it had been years and years ago. He felt a stabbing sense of regret, wishing he had spent more time with Catherine, but she had left the next afternoon.

Jacob looked over and saw Greta now crouching before an open cabinet, seeming motionless, frozen. She slowly stood up, her stockings bunching at her knees, and said she could find nothing there. He told her he had come across a carton of eggs in the refrigerator.

Over a dinner of warmed French bread and scrambled eggs, he first talked about the snow, which he believed would not accumulate, then he asked Greta about her family, and finally he spoke about the latest news back home. She was not overly responsive. Whenever she answered, she would look away, her eyes fixing on the small brass chandelier above the table. Had he offended her in some way?

After they finished eating, Greta stood and started to pick up the plates from the table but Jacob got up and said, "I'll take care of it." When he took the dishes from her, he saw that her hands were not steady.

"Excuse me," she said and he silently watched her wavering form as she made her way out of the room and soon heard her footsteps on the stairs. He was struck by her strength.

"I think I'll call my friend," he faintly called after her.

At the sound of Royce's voice, Jacob was filled with emotion. His friend's tone was the same as if Jacob were facing him—raspy but at the same time extraordinarily clear, like a willful and brazen auctioneer. It was late afternoon in the United States. Royce was on the East Coast, broadcasting his radio show from New York for the week.

"Who is she?" Royce asked.

Jacob shrugged, "I'm not certain," he answered in a low voice.

"You are not certain," Royce repeated. To Jacob his voice was both needling and sincere.

"No—not exactly," Jacob said, pouring more wine into his glass, explaining in more detail how he had met Greta, his first impression of her—young and old at the same time—the scare at the café, speaking over the phone with her friend Tommaso Rigoletti, his name, almost like the opera, a Florentine, a museum guide. Then he remembered he had picked up Tommaso's ring when Greta had dropped it onto the carpet. He touched his pants pocket and felt a small bulge, his fingers pressing into the hard ring.

There was silence and for a moment Jacob thought the connection had been broken. Then in a rush, Royce, his voice strained, said, "Catherine . . . can't believe it, Jake," sounding more solemn than Jacob had ever known him to be.

Jacob felt himself choking up; through his emotions, intense and suffocating, a hazy image came to him of Catherine handing Royce a note. At the time he had not focused on it; he had been more overjoyed by both Royce's and Catherine's presence, having them alongside each other—weren't they his two favorite people in the world?

"Was it simply an accident?" Royce asked in a soft raspy voice.

"Accidents are never simple," Jacob answered brusquely, recalling with disquietude how he had used those very same words with his mother. Then he took a long sip of wine and said. "Some things can't be changed, can't be fixed, but you want them to be—you ask yourself what steps you could have taken to prevent what happened, even long before the accident."

He didn't want to speak more of Catherine—it was overwhelming to do so—but neither did he want to end his conversation with Royce. If he did, any sense of hope would fade away.

Gingerly, Royce began to talk about a mutual college friend whom he'd bumped into the previous day in New York, on Broadway, coming out of the theater. And Jacob was relieved the conversation had been diverted from Catherine. But as Royce spoke about this friend, where he was working, that he had been recently married, and how he had inquired after Jacob, Jacob had a longing to ask Royce if he had seen Catherine again, before she traveled back to the West Coast the next day. But whenever he tried to break into Royce's words, his heart began to race. He pictured Catherine that evening, how in her swift yet languorous way she had got up from her chair, pausing for a moment before walking away, assessing him and Royce, her eyes bemused, the beauty spot between her eyebrows barely visible. Then she seemed about to sigh but stopped herself; she pushed back her hair with her right hand, waved good-bye with her left, and strode out into the night. It was the last time he had seen her move. Deeply pained now, he needed to catch his breath. And he was relieved when Royce continued to talk about this so-called friend whom Jacob barely remembered.

Once he felt grounded again, he thought of Greta lying upstairs in the other bedroom. He believed in her as he would have trusted any one of Catherine's more reasonable friends.

He looked out the French doors and saw that the snow was piling up. "We may be snowed in tonight," Jacob said, breaking into Royce's diatribe about New York—what he liked and didn't like about the city.

"What about your guest?" Royce asked sharply.

"She'll have to wait it out with me."

How much time had he and Royce spent together since they had graduated from college fifteen years before? What was Royce's life like in Los Angeles?

"Thanks for getting this place for me, Royce. It helps to be away." Jacob got up and began to pace. The snowfall was becoming more and more dense.

"I understand how difficult it must be losing a sister, losing Catherine," Royce said with a warmth Jacob had never before heard in his friend's voice, a warmth that nearly startled him.

He stopped pacing and went over to look again at the copy of the de Kooning painting; it struck him that the figure's expression was more like Catherine's than Greta's. Wasn't that the look Catherine had had on her face that night at the bar with him and Royce?

"That incident in the café—it must have been jarring for you and her," he now heard Royce say, breaking into his thoughts.

"It was shocking, but it happened so fast—it was like a tornado that had just missed us and then struck a pastry shop a few streets over."

There was silence and then Jacob, his heart pounding, felt the blood rush to his face; he spoke before realizing what he was about to say. "How did you know Catherine, Royce? She handed you a note that night at the bar." He felt himself sinking within—he couldn't move, couldn't take his eyes off the painting.

Quietly, evenly, Royce said, "Your mind is foggy, it is understandable."

"No, Royce, my mind has never been more clear."

"Go to sleep, Jacob. You are tired, overwrought. You've been through too much. You need to sleep."

"*Sleep*—don't you know, I am already numb."

He suddenly felt free to move and again began to pace. "You are ignoring my question, Royce."

"Even in death your sister deserves her privacy."

Jacob felt as if he were about to lose his balance. Abruptly he sat down on the sofa. He shuddered. "I've lost so much, Royce," he said, knowing he did not sound at all regretful or angry, but accepting, and that was what bothered him most. Wasn't acceptance simply a snare?

From the bedroom she heard Jacob downstairs, his words like murmurs, one sound indistinguishable from the next, lingering into the evening, like a breeze whispering into a summer night, soothing the back of her mind as she lay awake. Before getting into bed she had slipped out of her dress. As her bare chest brushed the large white pillow, it was if she were a child again and it was her mother below in the living room, talking on the phone with one of her friends. But it was December, not July, and although the heat was on, there was a chill in the air, and the bedroom window was partly obscured by snow. She was an adult now and it wasn't her mother's voice she heard, but the vague and uneven tone of Jacob's, a stranger. She closed her eyes, recalled what had happened at the café in Paris and shivered—it was beginning to pervade her sense of reality. Because of this event she was in a French town outside of Paris, a place she had not before heard of, with an unfamiliar person, in a bed not intended for her. Sharply her thoughts turned to Florence—how she had left so abruptly. She felt a deep sense of guilt, straining to remember what had happened moments before Tommaso had been struck by the car—but she couldn't, it was all a blur. All she knew was that the accident had occurred. Yet clearly she recalled the long train ride from Florence to Paris and how stunned she'd felt, unable to fathom how she had managed to pack, then get herself to the station and on the train.

Restless, she turned and lay on her back, pressing the blanket to her throat, hoping to hear what Jacob was saying, needing to know more about him, but the more she tried, the more exhausted she became—she was too far from him, his voice was too low.

Flashes of Tommaso crossed her mind—Tommaso at the Uffizi, explaining the Venus in great detail, his eyes serious and intent, his raised hand parallel to the canvas, pointing out aspects of the painting he found most compelling; Tommaso, joking after a lecture, telling the group to ignore his words whenever his descriptions sounded intellectual—for if they were, he most definitely was off-key. And then he smiled as if he were confused by his own words. She pictured Tommaso smoking a cigar, the sweet and acrid smell of the tobacco—Tommaso standing in front of the bedroom mirror naked, his face somber. And that chilly mid-November afternoon when she had unexpectedly come upon Tommaso eating at a small restaurant with wooden benches and a red tablecloth, the collar of his coat turned up, his shoulders hunching forward. She had come up behind him, wanting to wrap her body around his. He must have felt her presence, for suddenly he turned to her, looking at her as if he understood her, who she was. And that had been the beginning—she was the one he had wanted to be with, not any one of the others.

But soon she fell asleep and first dreamed not of Tommaso but of Jacob, his eyes glued to the ring on her finger, as they walked down the Champs-Élyseés. He held her hand then brought her finger to his lips, the one adorned with Tommaso's ring. Not paying attention to where he was going, he slipped, and they both fell to the ground, pedestrians passing by, some stepping over them. They couldn't get up, crying out for help with their arms extended, but people ignored them as if they were invisible. And then out of the blue appeared Tommaso, but suddenly she and Jacob were at a restaurant eating lunch huddled together because it was cold—and when he looked up from his plate, he was no longer Jacob but Tommaso. As she cried out, she heard a knock at the door. Was this knock part of her dream or was it real? She felt herself coming out of her sleep, opened her eyes, lifted her head from the pillow.

"Yes?" she asked in a whisper.

Jacob opened the door slightly and peeked his head into the room, his eyes hesitant and weary. "Just checking to see if all is well," he said quickly.

Had she cried out? Had he heard? Had she said a name—one or the other?

"May I come in?" he asked. She nodded and he came to the table beside her bed and she watched him drop Tommaso's ring onto it.

"How are you?" he asked.

"I'm okay," she said sleepily, sitting up.

His mouth gaped open, his dark eyes eerily still. But it was not until she recognized fear in his expression, his lips moving but no sound coming from him, she realized her chest was bare. As she abruptly covered herself with the blanket, he turned away and was silent. Then he looked back at her, their gazes meeting. Again she saw fright in his eyes. He raised his hand as if he were about to reveal something to her, something that had been worrying him, she thought. But he didn't; he shook his head as if he were both scared and puzzled and left the room, shutting the door. Soon she heard his footsteps descending the stairs.

Tears came to her eyes. Shaken by his response, her heart thumped. She got out of bed and put on her dress—she wanted to leave. But when she looked out the window she saw snow falling heavily. Pressing her forehead to the pane, all she could see was white—no trees, no pond, not one house—only white.

She switched on the light and for the first time looked about the room. The wallpaper was a medium blue with yellow bands. In the attached bathroom there was a long vertical mirror in a brass frame and when she caught her image she was surprised—her eyes were red and her lids dark. Her face looked thin and angular. Immediately, she turned to switch off the light, then got back into bed wearing her unzipped dress, pulling the covers over her head.

Sobbing, she pressed her face into the pillow. She had never felt more alone. She and Jacob could have been killed in the café, she thought, and began to shake. "Tommaso," she cried out.

If only her mother had come to Paris. She recalled all the times her mother had not shown up when she had said she would—her high school tennis tournaments, a movie or dinner with a friend and her parent. And she thought of how as a young girl she'd come home after school and often find her mother at the kitchen table, sitting with her shoulders erect, her back straight, her eyebrows knit, her face expressionless, drawing with exactitude on her thick art pad the likeness of whatever stood or lay on the table before her—a single rose, a ceramic vase, a candle with a glowering flame. At these moments she had been struck by the rigidity of her mother's posture—it was unnatural—but at the same time it was how Greta had come to understand there was more to life than what was in front of her, than what she saw and heard.

Home—she didn't know what she would do when she returned—the word had ceased to have any meaning for her. She did not belong there. Her thoughts rapidly turned to her life in college, her roommate Elaine, and then Florence—that late October night Elaine unexpectedly had come to her room. Greta had heard a knock at the door, and had known immediately it was Elaine's knock, firm, determined. When Elaine walked in Greta was in her robe, having just come from the shower; at first glance she saw Elaine's cheeks were flushed.

Elaine was in a nightgown that covered her neck; it was a nightgown a young girl might wear, with pink hearts around the bodice. But the excitement in Elaine's face was anything but girlish.

Elaine approached her, touched her arm, looked her directly in the eye, her expression intense, her face drawn. "I'm in love with him, with Tommaso," she said, her dark eyes steady, her chin raised. There was a harsh beauty to her, Greta thought—that was what passion had evoked in her. No longer was she the brash yet dreamy person she had known for the last four and a half years. For the first time since she had met Elaine, she fully believed her. But she derived no enjoyment from Elaine's words as she had in the past, in their college dormitory room, where she would listen to her friend recount her so-called adventures, exaggerations mostly, and her dreams; instead Greta felt as if a tiny, piercing dart had struck her chest.

"What happened?" she asked, her throat so dry she had to force out the words.

"Nothing happened," Elaine responded, tightly grasping the bedpost. "Nothing has to happen, it is just there, he is just there. It is not as I thought it would be."

"What is not as you thought it would be?" Greta asked, hearing the tension in her voice.

"So you love him too," Elaine said, lowering her gaze. She turned away and left the room.

But the next day it was as if she had not had that conversation with Elaine; it might as well have been a dream. Elaine was her usual self, and behaved toward Tommaso as she had done in the past, in a teasing, sisterly way.

As Greta now lay in bed and watched the snow fall, she hoped this was how it would be tomorrow with Jacob—as if nothing had happened, as if his coming into her room and seeing her bare chest had been a figment of her imagination.

As she fell asleep, she dreamed again of Tommaso—he was outside her window, frolicking in the snow. But upon peering down again, she saw it was no longer Tommaso but her mother and father, smoking marijuana. When she awoke, her eyes were wet with tears. Slowly adjusting to the darkness, she looked about the room; the window pane was fully covered with snow and she could not see out of it. Silence. She lay still in her bed, clutching the blanket close to her for warmth.

Jacob, disquieted by his reaction to Greta, descended the stairs, feeling a growing sense of shame—how ineffective he'd been in his attempt to communicate his vulnerability to her.

He left the kitchen light on and turned off the others. In near darkness he went up to the French doors and peered out at the snow piling up. All he saw was white, like a blank movie screen, and as best he could he envisioned the night at the bar with his sister and Royce as if it were a fuzzy scene playing out before him.

Like a director, he imagined the set—rectangular wooden tables, a long bar off to the left, a high-beamed ceiling. He and Royce seated on either side of Catherine, at a table situated toward the center of the room. And it was as if from a hazy distance he were observing his old self—confident, expressive, chuckling, his body leaning forward.

That night Catherine had been less talkative than usual, more restless, crossing and uncrossing her legs, running her small hand up and down one side of her glass of beer. At the time he could not tell if she had been paying much attention to the conversation; she seemed preoccupied with other thoughts. From time to time her gaze would wander to Royce. But there was no response from his friend—he didn't appear at all daunted by her presence, but Jacob had noticed how Royce had shifted his chair toward Catherine.

He wished he'd been more aware that night, instead of pushing away any questions about the two of them that had come to mind, preferring to bask in the presence of the two people he deeply valued.

There was Catherine before their drinks had been served, her narrow elbows on the table, her fingers resting on either side of her face, her pale hair falling over her hands, lifting her eyes from time to time, looking bemusedly at Royce, as if she knew him, as if she wanted to say something about it to Jacob. And Royce next to her, smiling in that broad way of his, unconcerned and comfortable because no matter where he was he'd always been that way. But Jacob's attention had been focused more on his sister, every move she made, every look she gave, and yet in another way he had taken her presence for granted. At certain moments he wondered if she were about to divulge something to him—her lips parted, her gaze fastening on his.

He winced, frustrated by what had not been said and what now could never be said, and turned away from the French doors. Not wanting to awaken Greta, he removed his shoes and awkwardly crept up the stairs. As he opened his bedroom door, he thought of Greta—how he had felt nothing, he had looked at her for only a moment—a glance—but he'd taken it all in, the shape, the size, the fullness, but most poignantly, he'd asked himself if the sight of a woman's breasts no longer moved him. He'd been like an architect without a measuring tape, making mental calculations. How hopeless this made him feel, how vacant. Furtively he had looked at magazines as a boy with his friends, photos of naked women with voluptuous tanned breasts.

As he paced about the bedroom he realized it was still snowing, a steady endless fall—the kind he hadn't seen since boyhood, or maybe hadn't noticed since then, one that could go on for days.

Once he had left home and gone to college, he'd been too busy to notice much—he'd been an athlete and had spent most of his spare time with other athletes, not one of them seeming to focus on anything other than how well one played, how well one swung a bat, how well one threw a curve ball. On the whole they had been critical of other students not in their circle—at first women too; not one was good enough, attractive enough. But that hadn't lasted long as one by one they became enamored with a Kristina, or a Jessica, or a Colleen. These friends of his had not paid much heed to the trees surrounding the baseball field or the greenness of the grass, and neither had Jacob. For any attempt of his to appreciate nature had slowed him down, emptied him, whether it be a stunning sunset or driving down a highway and unexpectedly spotting a majestic mountain in the distance. His indifference to such phenomena had continued until now. Confined in this townhouse in a foreign country, he was compelled by the steady snow, how it fell ceaselessly, as if not taking a breath to stop. He went to the window, pushed aside the drapes, pressed his palms against the pane, and stood there, transfixed. Camus's words came to him: "In the midst of winter, I found there was, within me, an invincible summer." And he felt a glimmer of hope.

But then Jacob's thoughts flashed to Greta, how she had sat up in bed, her breasts innocently exposed, and how he had been afraid. He banged the palms of his hands against the glass, not angrily but assertively. It never had been easy for him to admit his fears—he'd had no reason to before Catherine's accident. Of course he'd had them from time to time. Once he'd been running a campaign in a southern state, a governor's race, and someone had asked him what the candidate's view on capital punishment was—he had not known, he was new to the campaign, he'd just taken over from the previous manager who'd been fired, and had not bothered to find out. His mind went blank—and he was tied up in knots and didn't know what to say. He was afraid then because he'd always relied on his ability to respond. That was what had got him through things, his ability to talk, to answer, clearly, decisively, convincingly—as in college he had been able to react naturally to a pitched ball, at least until he'd been injured and could no longer drive it out of the park.

After graduation from college, he worked for a few years as a fundraiser for a variety of charitable organizations. It didn't take him long to realize this wasn't the right fit for him, and soon afterward he turned to politics, using the same ability to react—now verbally—that had always served him well. But that one moment when he'd been asked the question about capital punishment on a rainy July afternoon in the deep south, he'd been tongue-tied and afraid—it was one of the few times he hadn't done his homework.

Whether or not he completed his schoolwork was not a question his parents had ever asked—they took his diligence for granted; they were each preoccupied with their own careers, their own interests. And he thought of the day he'd seen a stranger leave their home as his father steered his BMW into the driveway. Jacob had been coming up the street and saw the front door slowly open, noticed a man's strong hand on the knob. Reflexively he ran and hid behind the bushes in the side yard. He was eleven at the time. His heart raced. From his hiding position, the branches bristling against his face, he watched as his father and this unknown man passed each other on the front path. Uneventful. And so Jacob had assumed the man was someone his mother worked in tandem with, someone who was a freelance journalist like herself.

Because of his parents' busy work schedules, he had taken it upon himself to watch over Catherine. But he had done so in a no-nonsense way. On those March vacations in the Caribbean, every afternoon at four, his parents would disappear inside a grass hut, beads hanging down the entrance way, to have a drink or two. He'd bring Catherine out onto the beach and tell her not to cry when she demanded to see their mother. "Don't be a baby," he'd say. "She and Dad are relaxing—they work a lot, they need a vacation, let me race you to the water." But he didn't always let her win; there were times, more often than not, he won the race. Once his friend from middle school had accompanied them on a trip and had chided Jacob for not letting his sister win the race to the ocean. Jacob had simply shrugged, thinking his friend was naive. With such parents Catherine needed to be toughened up. She could not afford to be thin-skinned. But no matter how much he tried, he never was able to curb Catherine's sensitivity, and eventually he stopped trying.

Another image of Catherine that night in the bar now floated through his mind. It was soon before she left—still seated, no longer restless, her hands on her lap, she'd gazed over at Royce—her expression was as serene and detached as that of the woman in the de Kooning painting.

Overcome with sorrow, he let his gaze rest on the bed; he thought now of Greta, her bare breasts, the color draining from her face—quickly, he left his room and went to her door.

For a short time Greta slept. When she awoke, she recalled not one dream, but was gripped with a sense of panic. Her heart was racing, she needed to know whether or not Tommaso was alive. She looked up at the swirls on the ceiling, crusty and white like the snow covering the window. Suddenly she heard a hollow thumping sound coming from another room. Snow falling from the roof and hitting a windowpane? After a few minutes there was silence.

She sat up and looked across the room, waiting for her eyes to adjust to the darkness. Her phone was on the bureau. She threw off the covers and got out of bed to fetch it. When she turned it on, it lit up in the darkness. She switched on the lamp and brought the phone back to bed with her. It was close to three o'clock in the morning. She checked through her messages—text and email—but there was nothing. At a loss, she recalled Tommaso saying to her only one week before: "Greta, you must not be shaken by what you do not expect."

They had been walking past the Uffizi. It was raining, a steady, cold drizzle. After he spoke, Tommaso opened his umbrella and held it over them. He wore a black raincoat, and his blond hair was slightly wet; effortlessly he brushed falling strands to the side. Greta heard his ring clacking against the handle of the umbrella.

She stopped walking, turned to him and asked, "Why are you saying this now, Tommaso?" She'd heard annoyance in her voice—she knew he could be dramatic in his speech whenever he wanted to provoke a conversation between them, bring something up that was on his mind. But at the time she was cold and longed to be indoors, whether it be at a café or her room; she wasn't drawn in by his words.

"You are not very happy, Greta," he responded, his lips tightening. "You don't like me saying this. It is not something you are ready to hear?"

Spontaneously she embraced him, held him close, resting her head on his shoulder, the dampness from his coat caressing her face. "I am happy, Tommaso, never doubt that." But his expression had been downcast.

Now a chill ran through her; it was as if he'd had a premonition about what was to happen. Unexpected, but perhaps not fatal, she thought. And she felt more hopeful—maybe he wasn't critically hurt from the accident, maybe the car had not directly hit him, maybe he would be all right. But she'd have to wait to know the truth.

Slowly tears fell down her cheeks. She held the blanket close to her face. Her thoughts turned to Jacob—she knew he wouldn't come in again.

In the fog that exists between sleep and consciousness, things can transpire—she knew this only too well. She thought of that time in college, after a late study group, she and Steve—all she'd known at the time was his first name, for she had not spoken to him before that night though she had found him attractive and had been curious to know more about him. In class he had been quiet, and she had sensed there was something mysterious about him. His hair was never fully combed, his eyes gray and wandering, and he was the first one to leave the room once class ended. That night after the others had gone back to their dorms, they had stayed behind in the student lounge. It was very late and they were too tired to move. The lights went out, and they began to doze off. Twenty minutes later, emerging from their sleep, they had reached out to each other, touching, exploring. But with Jacob earlier this evening, nothing had happened—she was relieved yet hurt by how abruptly he'd gone away.

Now she looked again at her phone, wanting to try Tommaso's cell number again—but it was much too early.

Her thoughts drifted again to her experience with Steve and their very short relationship. At the end of the semester, he had invited her to dinner at the best restaurant in their small college town. She didn't know why she had agreed to go—they had stopped seeing each other a month before. But what she most remembered about that night was walking into the restaurant with him as if he were a shadow at her side, and how as they stood in the foyer, waiting for a table, her eyes had met those of a woman coming from the dining area. And at that moment her heart began to beat quickly—the woman resembled in every way the mother of one of her friends from the city where she'd grown up—her deep blue eyes, her height and sturdy figure, her complexion, the length and blond color of her hair, the shape of her face and how she raised her eyebrows—Mrs. Cadence, someone who'd been kind to her, someone who had often come into her parents' shop to buy cards. But when this woman who resembled her friend's mother looked at Greta, she showed no sign of recognition because she wasn't Mrs. Cadence, she was just someone who bore an exceptionally strong resemblance to her. The more Greta stared at her in disbelief, the more the woman's gaze grew angry, then suspicious. It was eerie to experience a look of nonrecognition and distrust from someone whom you believed because of her appearance should have known you well. And Greta recalled the print of herself on the card in her parents' shop. When she first saw it, she had experienced the same strange feeling—one of recognition and nonrecognition at the same time.

Greta thought maybe it wasn't because her likeness had been distorted through the printing process but perhaps it was because that was how she appeared—bland and unreadable. Troubled, she closed her eyes, and heard a quiet knock at the door.

When she opened the bedroom door, Jacob forced himself to smile, noting how adroitly she avoided his gaze. He apologized for disturbing her at three o'clock in the morning—with a crack in his voice, he mentioned his rudeness earlier, leaving her room so abruptly. Speaking in this way, he was at times uneasy but on the whole felt painfully justified. Once he finished, Greta nodded, her eyes still cast away, her shoulders slightly raised. Then slowly, almost graciously, she shut the door, closing him out. He stood in the hallway facing the closed door for a few minutes, imagining her crawling back into bed still in her dress with the zipper at the back mostly undone.

In his room, Jacob lay in the dark, unable to sleep, his arms folded behind his head. From time to time he'd turn his gaze to the window; a small part of the pane, like an enlarged peep-hole, was not yet covered with flakes. Looking through it, he noticed the uninterrupted flow of falling snow, not straight but slanted, just like his life. And crossing his mind was an image of himself sliding off a shiny dark-brown horse on a merry-go-round and how his father had scooped him up just before he hit the platform. The oversized cowboy hat on his head caused him to feel off balance; he had raised his shoulders, tilting them, to keep the hat in place. Four years old, his legs had been long for his body. Just before he got on the plastic horse, his mother had snapped a photo of him, and as she did so she motioned with her hand for him to push back his hat, telling him she wanted to see his face. And he had followed her instructions, later believing this was why he'd not been able to balance himself on the horse. Bemusedly, she would call it "the day Jake fell off the pony," as she'd reach to take the framed photo from the shelf and languidly pass it on to an inquisitive visitor or friend who had noticed it and had asked to look at it up close.

Three years later, Catherine was born. The long, soft blanket she was wrapped in caressed him as he held his infant sister in his lap for the first time, the babysitter sitting close by. Unexpectedly his foot got tangled in the material; agitated, he tugged at it to free himself. As he was about to fall off the sofa with Catherine in his arms, Dorothy, their babysitter, protectively wrapped her arms around him as all three glided safely to the floor, his sister still in his arms, Dorothy next to him, encircling them.

Dorothy was in her early thirties and divorced, taking courses at night to complete her college degree. She was thin and had long brown hair that fell to her waist; her expression was mostly solemn, her dark eyes intense, her movements lithe. He interpreted her seriousness as sadness. And as young as he was he wondered if she wished she had children of her own. But she'd smile whenever he told her how beautiful she was, the most beautiful person he'd ever seen. With his seven-year-old perspective, he thought this was true, especially when she broke into laughter. For when she did so she'd toss back her head, her hair flowing down her back, her small forehead seeming to glisten and expand, and he'd feel gratified. He began to relish his role of entertainer, the first role he'd had that had meant something to him; he'd helped someone he had thought of as sad, be happy.

By the time he turned twelve, he realized his family was not the same as those of his friends. At first he was not able to put his finger on exactly what is was that made them different—it was just a feeling he had. He was vaguely aware that families of his friends spent weekends going to sporting events or movies together, whereas his did not.

There was a neighbor, a woman with a dog, who lived diagonally across from them. Superficially she reminded him of his mother—she was tall like his mother but not as slim, and moved in the same slow and exacting way. Her hair was a white-blond color, a few shades lighter than his mother's. He thought she lacked his mother's warmth. Adrienne was her name—it is what she had asked Jacob to call her. She'd phone and ask him to walk her dog. Not only did she pay him well, but on certain days she'd also hand him as a bonus four or five chocolate bars in a cloth pouch, laced with the scent of her perfume. Her dog was a miniature French poodle named Fleur. Jacob often felt uncomfortable walking her; he believed his friends would tease him if they saw him with a leash in hand either trailing or leading such a tiny dog. One day he noticed two friends of his in the distance coming toward him. Knowing they had not yet recognized him, he took an abrupt left onto a side street, and then took the back route to Adrienne's home, looking over his shoulder most of the way.

Coming up the front path sooner than usual, he heard Adrienne's slow drawling voice. It was a warm day in early May and all her front windows were open, the drapes flowing. Through an open window, Jacob saw her pressing a white phone to her ear, leisurely pacing before the front stairway in the foyer. She was wearing a long-sleeved, loose, white silk blouse over matching pants. He heard her say his mother's first name, but did not realize it was his mother she was speaking of. Then she spoke of his father, how darling of a man he was and how she hoped the son—meaning him, Jacob—would take after him and not the devil-may-care mother. "She has no shame," Adrienne said. "And her husband so very, very attractive—it is rather stunning." Jacob felt something within himself drop like a rock. Was it his heart falling to his stomach? And how sweaty his hands were, the dog's leash nearly slipping from his grasp. Then silence: she had suddenly stopped talking as he realized she must have noticed him approaching the house. Before he reached the top step, she had opened the door. He picked up Fleur and handed her to Adrienne, then turned away. "Wait, Jacob," Adrienne said in a commanding voice. He froze. Then he looked back and saw she had put Fleur down on the floor of the foyer. Within seconds Adrienne was embracing him, pressing his head into her silk blouse, her breasts surprisingly soft and round, the smell of her perfume filling his senses. And Jacob felt a stirring of desire that frightened him. He jiggled himself free. Running home, he heard Fleur's yapping bark.

Never before had he been more confused. For the next few weeks, whenever his father was inside his home office, Jacob would stand outside the door, wanting to knock, go in, and tell his father about what he had overheard Adrienne say. One day, his father had abruptly come out, nearly running into him. "What's wrong, Jake?" He knew his father was startled to see him standing so close to the door, especially since Jacob rarely confided in him. They shared a quiet relationship, an easy one—although their temperaments were different, they understood each other intuitively. But seeing his father look so puzzled was disorienting. Jacob turned away, and as he did so he felt his father's grasp on his shoulder. "What is it, Jake?" his father asked solemnly, not taking his hand away. When Jacob turned and met his father's gaze, he remembered Adrienne's words about his father's attractiveness, and for the first time he became aware of it, the warm chestnut brown eyes, now concerned, his dark, thick hair, his full lips, and it dawned on Jacob why he hadn't before noticed his father's appearance—it was because his father himself had not been conscious of it; his father was not vain.

Jacob went inside the office, watching as his father turned the lock on the door. They sat next to each other on the beige leather sofa. And then it was as if something let loose within Jacob, and in a steady but heavy voice he poured out to him what he had heard Adrienne say. His father's expression of puzzlement turned to concern, his jaw tightening. Jacob wasn't certain if he saw tears in the corners of his eyes. "Everyone's marriage is different," he said slowly, thoughtfully. "Jacob, you mustn't care what others think. We love you and that is all that matters." Jacob felt as if he'd been stabbed—in speaking this way his father was confirming what Jacob had overheard about his mother. He recalled seeing the strange man coming out of their home the previous year, passing his father on the front path. Then Jacob felt another stab but this time it was anger—he was angry with all of them, his mother, his father, and Adrienne, whom he avoided from that day forward.

No longer was he or would he ever again be understanding of his father's temperament. And the growing estrangement he felt toward his mother bewildered him. How warm and endearing she could be at times. But there were other occasions when her eyes would widen a bit and become fixed, as if she were lost in thought, just when he believed she was fully engaged in what he'd been telling her. With his mother and father in a sense both now strangers to him, he was at a loss and so, after a month or two of attempting to come to grips with who his parents were, or had become, he began to feel more independent, more brazen. His sister Catherine noticed it first. "You are not very kind any more, Jake, you have a funny scowl on your face most of the time. You look as if you've swallowed something you didn't like the taste of."

He hesitated for a moment or two, but then regained his new self and said, "Come on, Cate, you are too thin-skinned."

And she responded, "Thin-skinned? I don't know what that means, Jake."

He looked away, thrust his hands in his pants pockets and said, "Forget it, it's not important."

"Why isn't it important? You said it." Her six-year-old face peered up at him. He gazed down at her wary expression; he was aware of her strong belief in him, and he felt a pang that nearly shook him.

"Do you think I've eaten a snake?" he asked with a smile on his face. And she brightened up and said with confidence, "You say funny things—you are the same Jake."

As he now looked toward the window and out at the darkness beyond the falling snow, his ankles crossed, his body beginning to relax, he thought of the day, a school vacation day, he'd brought Catherine to the museum. His mother had instructed him to do so, as she was tied up with her work. There had been many school vacation afternoons that his mother had sent him and Catherine off to the museum or to the movie theater. On this day he must have been fifteen, and Catherine eight. He vaguely recalled how they had wandered into a special exhibit, and how his sister, pointing to the nude statue of a warrior, had asked, "What is that, Jake? I've never seen that before." Her mouth was open, her eyes fixed on the statue. For a moment he thought she seemed older than her age, and he felt himself blush. Immediately, he tried to control his embarrassment, chiding himself for having blushed even when he hadn't been certain what she was referring to—the private parts on the marble figure or the sword in the statue's hand?

His voice abrupt, he said to her, "You are still young, Catherine, there are lots of things you haven't seen yet, but you'll have your chance. You just have to grow up a little bit first." Then she reached up as if to touch the marble statue, her small finger pointing to the genitals. "No, you can't touch, Catherine," he whispered. "It is not a person, it is marble."

She turned and looked at him and said, "Jake, I know it is not real," her eyes looking at him in hurt disbelief, as if he had underestimated her. He didn't know how to respond to her or what to say; he just nodded and took her hand, leading her away from the statues into another room.

It struck him now they might have looked at de Kooning's *Seated Woman* that day—was it because the print downstairs had jogged his memory? Or had it been another time? Hazily he recalled Catherine in front of the painting, silent, her face reddening, her shoulders dropping. Then, turning away from it, her cheeks still flushed, she looked up at him and said defiantly, "I know her." And Jake had thought of his mother and what Adrienne had said about her. Then he remembered the previous March, coming home and finding Catherine sitting in the middle of the kitchen floor, holding tightly onto her stuffed panda bear. A mother of a friend of hers had driven her home from school—they'd been dismissed early because of flooding in the gymnasium. Catherine had looked up at him, her expression fearful, and said she did not know where their mother was, she'd heard a voice coming from upstairs, one she did not know. Immediately he had taken her by the hand, walking with her out of the house, telling her he was bringing her to the ice cream shop.

These thoughts caused him to feel light-headed—so much so that he did not know where to go. "Are you alright, Jake?" Catherine asked, her tiny hand tugging at his wrist. "Your face has gone white."

"I'm fine," he insisted, again and again, until she stopped asking.

"I'm fine," he said aloud now in the same stunned way he'd said it to Catherine that day at the museum. But whom was he telling this to now—himself, or did he believe Catherine was some place where she could hear him? And was he fine? Maybe, he thought.

He reached for the remote control on the table next to the bed and switched on the television. They were speaking about another attack that had been aborted. Maybe the French were no longer as accepting of these attacks as he had believed, maybe they couldn't so easily go on with their lives as if nothing had happened. He had been deluding himself about the French as he'd been deluding himself about his own state. He was not fine, and might never be so again.

Another time he'd come upon Catherine unexpectedly. She was fifteen and he twenty-two. A small bookstore a few miles from their home—she was sitting in the café part of the shop. He had just graduated from college and had come in to buy a book to read. The next day he would be taking a flight to St. Louis for a job interview.

At first he did not recognize her. She wore her hair differently that day—two strands were braided and held back in a barrette, the rest flowing down her back. Her head was bent over a glass of lemonade, her mouth on the straw, her shoulders hunched. He walked over to her and said her name. When she looked up at him, he saw that her eyes were red. He sat in the empty seat across from her. "What is wrong, Catherine?" he asked. She did not appear surprised to see him, and blinked two or three times to control her tears. He turned his head away and asked if she'd like a ride home. For the previous few years or so he had felt uncomfortable whenever she cried. She had seemed too old to be doing so. There was a time when her tears had broken his heart, and he would have done anything to protect her, but he didn't feel that way anymore. He then heard her voice. It sounded stronger than he expected, lower too, as if she had just awakened from a long sleep. She told him to leave her alone. She could get home on her own. He nodded and got up. Although he was annoyed at Catherine for crying, he was uneasy about leaving her there.

Two weeks later he had gleaned she had been stood up by a boy that she liked. Passing by her bedroom, he had overheard her telling a friend about it over the phone. She didn't sound sad, but confident, disdainful of the boy. Apparently she had to a certain degree put it behind her. Or had she?

He had accepted the job in St. Louis, and his interactions with Catherine from that point onward—the last fifteen years—had been occasional, three, maybe four times a year, and short in duration. That afternoon at the bookstore café was the last time he'd seen her cry. And that same day he'd purchased a book on the political writings of Locke. He'd often joke that in college he'd had a double major—baseball and philosophy. But that afternoon he'd had a hankering to read Locke again, more thoroughly this time.

And now, turning his gaze to the window, he saw how the snow kept coming, he recognized how he had built up within himself over the years, layers and layers of humor and brusqueness, covering his concern for his sister and his confusion about his family as a whole. In doing so he'd been searching aimlessly for a way to center himself.

When he dozed off his dreams were scattered. His father riding a bike over a grassy path, wearing only a pair of sunglasses, his body surprisingly hairy, almost like an animal. His mother dressed in a long flimsy white gown, kicking off her shoes, resting her feet on the coffee table, her smile revealing her to be toothless. And then there was Catherine stuck in a snowbank, calling out his name, telling him she couldn't move. Surrounded by snowbanks, he didn't know which one she was in—he couldn't follow her voice. He told her to move, move Catherine, you can do it, and he felt himself becoming more and more frustrated with her. His frustration soon turned into pain as if he'd been kicked in the gut and then suddenly he woke up. For a moment he was not aware of where he was. Slowly it came to him—France, a snowstorm. He got up and opened the bedroom door.

Descending the stairway, he felt a draft of cold air. He was still dressed in his clothes from the previous day, now wrinkled and clinging. When he got to the foot of the stairs, he walked into the living area, to the French doors, and looked out at the snow. The duck pond was completely covered—for he did not know exactly where it was. The snow was no longer falling at an angle but was swirling downward. All he could see in the distance was white—fleetingly he thought of Adrienne's white silk blouse infused with the scent of her perfume, his head buried between her breasts.

Greta awoke with a creeping sense of dread. Morning light passed through the snow-padded pane, barely illuminating a copy of a dark-hued baroque painting. The black tiles in the adjacent bathroom and the heavy mahogany furniture were incongruous with the modern structure of the townhouse, contributing to her deep unease. She assumed Tommaso was dead, and was fearful of having her belief confirmed. And she was wary of facing Jacob again. It was his look of distaste that had mortified her. She had successfully avoided his gaze when he'd knocked on her door at three in the morning, not wanting to witness again his unsettling and troubled eyes. Lowering her eyelids, she tried to steel herself for the day before her. With a sigh, she reached for her phone she had left at the foot of the mattress and got out of bed. She intended to call her professor, thinking there was a slim chance she still may be in Florence. But before doing so she checked her email and was relieved to see a message from Beth. She got out of bed and held the phone close to read it.

Hello Greta—Not certain if you know Tommaso has been in an accident—was hit by a car the last night we were all in Florence. Naturally his mother is very distressed—her only child. He will be okay in that he will live—it was touch and go the past few days. So I waited to contact you and the others until I knew he would survive. I have decided to stay with him. Hopefully, he will walk again one day. I will take a leave of absence from the college to help care for him. As I am certain you have come to realize, Tommaso and I have had an off and on relationship since we met. But now he needs me. Beth

Greta's hand shook; the phone dropped from her grasp, knocking Tommaso's ring off the table and onto the rug. With her bare foot she frantically tried to crush the ring, but it was hard and indestructible. She looked toward the window; through her tears the snowy pane looked hazy and amorphous. She reached for the bedpost to steady herself, yearning to be back home. But where was home? She felt unanchored and lost. Were all those things Tommaso had told her untrue—his passion for her? His admiration of her independent nature? So American, he had said—people like you are what is best about your country. Beth and Tommaso had been involved from the start—how naive she'd been! Still clutching the bedpost, she wondered if she should go to Tommaso. Her knees were trembling, trembling with joy that he was alive, trembling with despair because he had chosen Beth. Or had Beth chosen him? Although most of the women in the group had a passable knowledge of his native language, it now struck her that Beth had been the only one he'd spoken to in Italian.

Her trembling began to subside and the more it did the more she realized as much as she had loved him and of course still did, she had no desire to see him with Beth at his side in the role of his hovering nurse. She felt a deep and painful sense of loss, but it wasn't only because of Tommaso. For it dawned on her she had been lost when she'd been with him. He had not been quite real to her—he had been who she had wanted him to be. She did not really know who he was. She only knew what he represented to her—his open-mindedness, his ability to enjoy life, his innate creativity, his natural appreciation and understanding of art—traits she had not before seen or experienced.

Clearly Beth and he needed each other for reasons she could not fathom. Why had she not been aware of it until now? When she had been with Tommaso there had been a subdued uneasiness on his part—it had been like hearing sounds in the middle of the night, uncertain if they were real or imagined. She thought how happy she'd been just a week before—her departure from Florence, though approaching, had not yet been a reality. She was convinced Beth had no idea about her relationship with Tommaso—if she had, she would have not sent Greta an email; she would have kept her out of the loop. So Tommaso had not told Beth—it would be their secret. Yet at the same time Beth's not knowing made their affair less true. Through her sadness, she smiled and picked up the ring from the rug. Tightly holding it, she realized it wasn't Tommaso who'd been dying all along, but something deep inside her.

She went to the sink, leaned forward, looked closely at her image in the mirror, and in her eyes saw the same blank expression her mother had depicted in the painting of her as a child. Vigorously Greta splashed water over her face as if to rid herself of it. Then she went to the bedroom door, opened it, and tiptoed down the stairs in her bare feet. As she descended, she saw Jacob had just come in from shoveling, his hair and eyelashes covered with snow. She shivered from the draft of cold air, and he smiled uncertainly at her. In the light of day, had the cold and the snow erased the previous evening?

But as he unbuttoned his coat, Greta noticed a certain tilt to his shoulders, a steadfastness and yet an awkwardness, and intuitively she knew he had remembered seeing her half-naked, had not found it distasteful, was remembering, and perhaps would never forget. And she felt a deep and overwhelming fondness for him.

She went up to him and wrapped her arms around his taut waist, rested her head against the hollow of his chest. At first she felt him stiffen, as if constricted by her touch. He tried to talk, his voice hoarse. "What is it, Greta?" But she did not answer and he didn't question her further. She knew he wanted her to release him. But she was stubborn; she kept holding on. Soon she felt his body slowly lose its tension, his knees touching her thighs; on the small of her back his hands began to feel less rigid, the muscles in his legs were unfolding. Slowly his arms began to relax, and then she felt his sigh. She looked up at him. But he was gazing out toward the French doors. He had a faraway look in his eyes as if he were trying to remember something or perhaps trying to forget. But she kept craning her neck, looking up at him until he gazed down at her. In a whisper, he said, "I'm too old for you, Greta."

Intuitively she knew what he meant; it wasn't necessarily his age he was referring to. He was speaking of his sadness.

"Maybe you are," she whispered back. But they only clung together more. Eventually they moved up the stairway and into his bedroom. Gingerly he touched her face, as if in doing so he was uncovering some sort of information she had been holding from him, something that would help him understand the world which he felt he had so misjudged and perhaps had been misjudged in as well. For he believed her face, her dispassionate yet thoughtful eyes, her flat chin and pointy lips, held the key to all that mystified him.

To Greta everything was happening in slow motion; it was as if she were underwater and moving toward the surface, fearlessly discarding her illusions along the way.

~

After another meal of scrambled eggs, they sat on the sofa cushions in front of the French doors, drinking wine. Slowly, between sips, she explained to him about Tommaso and Beth. When he had finished his third glass, he told her about his sister named Catherine who had been killed a while ago in a car accident. Then he spoke of Royce, showing her two pictures of him from an old phone. She nodded and did not tell him she could not clearly see Royce. She asked to look at a photo of Catherine, but he said he didn't have one with him or on either cell. When she showed him a picture of Tommaso on her phone, he looked stunned, she thought, but then she assumed it was his way of revealing jealousy.

Eventually they fell asleep on the cushions, their arms and legs intertwined. Above them hung *Seated Woman,* sensual and defiant, like Titian's *Venus of Urbino,* undoubtedly, more free. When they awoke a few hours later, it was no longer snowing.

Late October

Jacob pauses in his lecture, raises his weary eyes from his notes, surveying the classroom: twenty students before him from the ages of nineteen to forty-seven, sitting at narrow desks, nearly all taking notes on their computers—some appearing to do so indifferently, others assiduously. The one exception is a young woman in her late twenties; her mouth tightly closed, she holds a pencil in her left hand and whenever something seems to strike her, she writes it down in her notebook. Jacob's talk has been on Locke, how his writings influenced the Founding Fathers. He is not certain what the Founding Fathers mean to his students, especially the younger ones. He doesn't ask, doesn't want to be disappointed. And so he's emphasized the philosopher's ideas on identity, the self, which he believes his class may relate to more.

As he does every Friday afternoon, Jacob ends the lecture with a quote, a thought for his students to ponder over the weekend. Though he imagines there is an intensity in his eyes—as there is whenever he echoes Locke's words—his tone is tempered: "Every man has a property in his own person. This nobody has a right to, but himself."

He smiles almost sheepishly at those before him. It is as eclectic a group as you can find, he thinks, watching carefully, but not overtly, as they gather their belongings and leave the room. As she walks out the door, he notices a more confident step in the nineteen-year-old who has a six-month-old child, and more strain in the face of the woman sitting in the first seat of the row farthest from the door, whose husband has been ill for the past year. Most have told him their stories.

If someone had predicted one year ago he'd be teaching at a community college with students from a myriad of backgrounds, he would have found it inconceivable. On some days he feels rejuvenated, happy to be away from the world of actual politics and campaigns, where one needs to twist the truth to such a degree it becomes a lie, malign those one respects in order to win. He is no longer able to view it like other political operatives do—as simply a game, no hard feelings. For he's come to realize the game is on the people, the innocent ones who are staunchly loyal to their ideology, whichever one it may be. Would they not be surprised at how well those in the higher echelons of opposing parties get along?

Teaching has soothed him, given him hope. Yet despite his general disillusionment with politics, on some days he has a surprisingly deep yearning for his life as it was, and his fervent belief that the deceptive part of politics was for the greater good. But after Catherine's unexpected death, and living with Greta—who has a natural albeit naive intolerance of politicians—for nearly a year, he has his doubts. Making compromises on your ethics, he has come to realize, is never for the greater good. And the greater good may be good for some, but never for all. Still, in certain ways, though he doesn't like to admit it, he longs for his past work, his past assumptions.

He is sharply aware and somewhat uneasy knowing that teaching at this community college affords him protection from who he was, from what he did. When he received a call this morning from a former colleague with an offer to go back to the world of politics, he was initially lured and felt a tug as he listened to the opportunity, his heart beating more quickly. He imagined himself advising, strategizing, intermingling with people on a campaign. But by the end of the conversation he said flatly that he would think about it, wondering if he would ever be ready to return to that life. For he's feeling too raw, too raw to know himself, to know what he wants, too raw to face the truth. All he has now is his relationship with Greta and yet she is not quite real to him—she is almost a figment of his imagination, one who appeared in his life when he was the most desolate. Now she prances around the periphery, with her natural diligence in whatever she sets out to do, talking from time to time about the future in a general way, peering into her computer screen, her body gracefully bending forward, like a dancer's, as if searching for some answer to what the next step in her life will be. And yet he's convinced she continues to live with him because she has no place else to go. He doesn't ask her about Tommaso; he hasn't since she told him he was involved with her professor. If she often thinks of Tommaso, he cannot tell. She isn't one to appear distracted or at loose ends. She is always focused, but her focus may be a shield. From time to time he vaguely wonders what she is hiding from.

In anticipation of Royce's visit, he leaves the college earlier today. He's cancelled his last class; he doesn't want to be late for his friend. As he makes his way across the campus to the lot where his car is parked, he notices one of his students from his last class, the woman in her late twenties, the one student who writes in a notebook. She is leaning against a stone sculpture at the edge of the campus. It is a modern and undecipherable piece with a ledge that looks like a shelf; he's seen other students use it as a place to put their books, or rest against before leaving for the day. She is smoking a cigarette in a leisurely way. She is smaller than he thought and he realizes he's only noticed her when she's been sitting at her desk. Amanda—that's her name, he recalls. As she seems somewhat bored in class, never showing any interest in his lectures, not taking part in class discussions, he's not paid much attention to her.

It has stopped drizzling and the sun is peeking out from behind the clouds, the golden late-October light falls suddenly across her shoulders, accenting the narrowness of her frame. He sees by the look of recognition in her eyes she's noticed him. Self-consciously she drops her cigarette to the ground and immediately covers it with her boot. He nods at her and she readily smiles. He is taken aback, not only by her openness—he's always thought of her as too contained, nonresponsive—but because her front tooth is markedly chipped. Yet, surprisingly, this irregularity does not detract from her appearance, but rather heightens it, adds another dimension to his perception of her. The sun goes back behind the clouds, a cold autumn wind gusts, and the fallen leaves fly upward and onto her shoulders, while the papers in her open pocketbook at her feet blow out of her bag and soon are covering Jacob's shoes. He bends to pick them up, and when he's standing straight again, he sees she's approaching him. He hands her the papers and she smiles, this time with her lips closed. Slightly lowering her head, she thanks him. Up close she appears pale, her small gray eyes are faintly outlined with mascara, her expression more present than in class, her cheeks too hollow for someone of her age. He wants to ask about her chipped tooth—he knows there is a story behind it. She is one of the few students in the class who's not told him about her life. As she walks away from him in a steady yet languorous way, he thinks of Catherine leaving the bar that night, the last time he saw her truly alive, giving a slight wave but turning away, determined to leave him alone with Royce. This woman possesses that same combination of strength and vulnerability. Shivering, he walks toward his car, reminding himself he hasn't seen Royce since that September night nearly fourteen months ago.

Inside, he turns up the heat and presses the button on the car radio to listen to the news. He comes in at the middle of a story; he gathers there has been another terrorist attack, a suicide bomber, but he cannot tell where it happened. From the announcer's impassive voice, he determines it is not in Europe or the United States; there is not the immediacy in his tone that there would be if the attack had been close. He assumes it happened far away, perhaps in Asia or in the far reaches of the Middle East. For the announcer has already switched to another story about a missing gibbon in a Floridian zoo who was later found drowned in a nearby lake. Jacob is unnerved by both stories, and thinks about the close call he and Greta had last year in the Paris café. How much has it influenced their relationship this past year? As it happened immediately after they met, he wonders what she was like before. He imagines she may have been more even-tempered, less anxious—but there had been Tommaso's accident as well. Then he thinks about Royce coming and how it will affect Greta, and about his own mixed and complicated feelings toward Royce. He recalls that snowy night in France with Greta—how she had leaned toward him with phone in hand, her eyes exceedingly pensive, showing him Tommaso's photo. Moments before he had pulled out his old cell so she could see Royce's picture, and prior to doing so he had told her as best he could about Catherine. He had known she had not been able to clearly make out Royce in the photograph, and he had not been completely honest about Catherine's accident, exactly when it had occurred.

He is stuck in traffic and it is only two fifteen. But it is Friday in Cambridge. He hears cars honking, sees gray clouds above, and within seconds rain splashes the windshield. He turns on the wipers, checks to see if his window is completely closed, then pushes the mute button to silence the radio.

And he is struck by the reality that he'll be seeing Royce in about two hours. He feels anxious. Not only is he uncertain about how Greta will respond to his friend, he is not sure what his own reaction will be, foreseeing questions he may impulsively ask Royce about Catherine. The traffic begins to move.

As he takes a right onto the street where they live, he spots Greta. Despite the rain, she walks slowly. Usually her step is fast-paced, swift, never slow-footed as it is now. He parks the car on the opposite side of the street, slides down his window, and calls out to her. She turns her head quickly. When her eyes rest on him, they widen in recognition and her lips curl into a slight smile. "Come on in so you don't get too wet," he calls out. The rain falls more steadily now.

When she gets into the car next to him, he feels he is more alive, the car inhabited, more electric, pleasant and unpleasant at the same time. The rims of her eyes are red and he wonders if she's been crying. She doesn't like to show that side of herself to him—she hasn't since they returned from Europe. He doesn't start the car; instead he puts his hand over hers and tells her about the call he received that morning from a former colleague in Philadelphia, about the possibility of going back there in the new year. It would be a job in the political world—he'd be more of an adviser, no longer in the trenches. But he does not know if he is ready to return to that life or if he ever will be. She impassively looks up at him and he takes his hand from hers and starts the car, drives down the street to their apartment. The sidewalks are mostly covered with damp leaves. She doesn't say anything, and he awaits her response, his heart beating rapidly. He is fearful she will tell him she will not go, that she does not want to leave her job or Cambridge. But she doesn't say that or anything else. As they drive into the parking lot next to the apartment building, he feels her looking at him but he does not meet her gaze. He wants to hear how she feels about it without any input from him. If she says no, he will not take it. He doesn't want to lose her—he does not know why. For he is not certain if their relationship has possibilities or not, if they are compatible or not—he just is not able to accept change in his life right now, change of an emotional kind. So he will hang on, will do whatever she wants. It seems as if her silence now is endless, it has been this way for hours, for days. He is surprised, as usually she has opinions about things, strong ones at times, uncertain ones at others, but she has never been hesitant about expressing herself.

As they climb the flight of stairs to their apartment, she turns to him on the step below her. She looks him fully in the eyes in that objective way of hers and rests her arms on his shoulders, fingering the collar of his raincoat, her lips lightly touching his.

It stopped raining an hour ago. The clouds have dispersed; fading light from a lowering sun filters through the sitting room windows, faintly spilling into the foyer of the apartment. As it is the last Friday of October, it is darker at four in the afternoon than it was one week before. Greta leans forward and presses the buzzer next to the door to let Royce inside the building. With a swelling sense of anticipation, she goes out into the corridor; her hands grasp the banister. A fixture hangs over the stairway, emitting a dim light. There is a familiar smell of onions; the neighbor in the next unit has begun her weekend cooking—from her CD player Greta softly hears a jazz pianist's rendition of "Happy Days Are Here Again." Jacob has remained inside, at his desk, preparing for his Monday classes.

Greta looks down and feels a chilly draft; Royce has just opened the main door of the apartment building. He stands in the foyer, his head down, his trench coat unbuttoned, revealing a very narrow yellow-and-brown striped tie. In his left hand he carries a worn briefcase. His hair is blond with streaks of brown, unevenly cut in the back. She is unable to see his features or expression as he does not look up; his gaze seems to be fixed on the old marble floor with small black-and-white square tiles. She straightens her posture, her shoulders erect, her knees touching the railing, her heart beating rapidly. Neither of them speak; she motions for him to climb the flight of stairs to the apartment. Because he nods without raising his head and begins his ascent, his head still down, she is certain he is aware of her.

She hears Jacob's footsteps and turns to him, faintly smiling. But he is gazing at Royce—his eyes are filled with restrained emotion. Then he glances at her; it is as if in some abstract way he is comparing them.

When she turns to fully look at Royce, she is startled and feels her face reddening—he so much resembles Tommaso! The weight of Jacob's hand presses against her shoulder, then it is no longer there. He's embracing Royce.

"It is as if I already know you," she says to Royce, her voice pressured, her eyes misty. They shake hands and she looks at him more closely. In his blue-green gaze—so much like Tommaso's—she perceives that behind it, wherein lies his inner self, he is not at all similar to Tommaso; his eyes are less expressive, suggesting he is more analytical and maybe less transparent. And she finds this even more painful than the resemblance—the lack of resemblance within the resemblance. She turns to

Jacob, who is leading the way inside the apartment. He knows, she thinks, recalling the night during the snowstorm in France when she had showed him Tommaso's picture, his strange reaction to it. This is why he was so strident yet detached in bed last night; he was worried about how she'd react to Royce. But comprehension does not lessen her surprise at the resemblance between Royce and Tommaso. She is withdrawn and thoughtful, not unlike a person who meets for the first time a relative who has been living abroad and who bears an uncanny resemblance to one's parent but whose essence is so very different, a print of the original.

Royce removes his raincoat; his movements are brisk, clipped. She feels uneasy in his presence; he dominates a room, becomes the center of it, just as Tommaso would. For a moment she longs for him to become Tommaso—she imagines his almost steely gaze, his detached yet sharp look turning warm, wistful, and slightly bemused.

Jacob crosses his legs, glances at her, gauging her impression of Royce. With a certain deftness Royce, sitting back in his chair, asks her questions about herself, about her present job, about where she grew up. His interest does not seem feigned, but mildly curious. He sits in the green-and-white plaid chair with his legs open then places his left ankle across his right knee and wiggles his foot. She can see how practiced he is at questioning people; it is his work, she reminds herself: he is a radio talk show host. She answers quickly, practically, not drawing attention to any part of her past or present life. He studies her for a moment, then smiles and turns to Jake, asks if he misses the world of politics.

Jacob shrugs and gets up, goes into the kitchen, and comes out with a bottle of Malbec. After he pours out the wine, they all lean forward and clink glasses.

Sharply, Greta's phone rings; she picks it up from the coffee table and sees it is her mother calling. She excuses herself and goes into the bedroom. Her mother, who has been careful not to interfere in her personal life, wants to know why she still hasn't met Jake—it's been ten months and they are living together. Because of her mother's restrained nature Greta has been able to avoid introducing her to Jake, but after ten months her mother has become surprisingly curious to meet him. "Next Sunday," she tells her mother with assurance—"one of Jake's friends is visiting this weekend."

When Greta returns to Jacob and Royce, she soon realizes they are talking about Jacob's sister Catherine. Greta feels uncomfortable, as if she is intruding, but does not know how to extricate herself—she wants to get up, leave the room, but does not know how to go about doing so. She wishes she had spoken more with Jacob about his sister, but he always seemed reticent to do so and so she never pursued it. She notices the forlorn expression now on Jacob's face—throbbing with sorrow. And she sees how restive Royce is: he stands up, walks over to the window, bending forward, he splays his hands over the sill and says how early it is to be so dark. Then Royce turns his head slowly toward Jacob and says he cannot believe it's been nearly a year since Catherine's accident. Greta feels startled. She drinks more wine. Jacob had led her to believe Catherine's accident happened some time ago. She experiences a strong sense of panic; her leg is shaking. For she has trusted Jacob as she has trusted no one else, not even Tommaso.

Her gaze now pointedly rests on Jacob; he doesn't turn to look at her.

She watches how Jacob shifts in his seat as Royce speaks about Catherine, and how he looks back at Royce with mild suspicion. The more they speak, the more they seem like strangers to her. Jacob has never expressed to her his grief about his sister. That is why he seemed so hesitant when she first met him.

Jacob stands up and says in a pleading voice that he is hungry. They decide to go out to dinner and start walking toward Harvard Square. She and Jacob are next to each other in the center of the sidewalk and Royce is a little apart, walking close to the curb, looking over at them from time to time. His step is almost jaunty and she feels a pang, thinking of Tommaso and how he would take that position when they were walking in a group. But there is something more grounded about Royce; he is not and probably will never be able to drop his guard.

It has grown colder, and, with their heads down, they hurry along without speaking.

At the restaurant Greta closely watches Jacob and Royce as they eat. Jacob knows the owner, who moved to Cambridge from Philadelphia. As their table is at the back, they do not feel the draft pervading the front of the restaurant. Instead, where they sit it is warm and toasty. Greta feels her cheeks reddening from the wine as she looks to see if Royce eats in the same way as Tommaso, but she can no longer recall Tommaso's mannerisms. She then imagines Tommaso in his apartment in Florence, Beth hovering close to him, her eyeglasses slipping to the end of her nose, reading aloud a piece about Vasari she'd found in an art magazine.

Greta feels light-headed; she no longer knows who Jacob is and at the same time Royce makes her less certain about Tommaso. Naturally they are different people. But their looks are so similar, there must be a connection, she tells herself, needing to hold on to this thought to help herself through the evening. Still uneasy from the shock of Royce's appearance and the shock of hearing that Jacob lost Catherine less than a year ago, most likely a few weeks before she met him in Paris, she tries to recall the exact words he had used in telling her about his sister. But Greta cannot remember Jacob's words, only his distant expression.

As they speak, she recalls Jacob in Paris, how withdrawn he seemed at first. And then his decision to teach political science at a community college in Cambridge instead of continuing on as a political operative—giving that up, it seemed, for good. Now she sees how the pieces fit into place and begins to feel a sense of comfort, an understanding of him. But her solace is short-lived—she reminds herself he was deceptive about his sister's death. Does he not trust her? And again she asks herself—who is Jacob? Who is Tommaso? It is as if Jacob and a Tommaso impersonator are sitting next to each other, across from her, facing her. Yet, isn't it Jacob and Royce, who are friends and in a sense partners, and she the stranger?

Why was she so compelled by Tommaso, and then Jacob? She looks over at Royce as if he holds the answer. But his expression is inscrutable. She comprehends only too well she is the only one who can know this.

Outside Royce's hotel, facing its red brick facade, they linger close to one of the two columns on either side of the entrance as they say good night. A strong, cutting wind sweeps by as Jacob, filled with conflicting emotions, soundly hugs Royce. When they separate, Jacob looks over at Greta, now leaning against one of the pillars. Her hands are deep inside the pockets of her coat, one foot impatiently toying with a small pile of damp leaves. She looks in the direction of the sliding glass door of the hotel, as if deciding whether or not to go inside. Their apartment is two blocks away. Royce rubs his hands together and asks, "Is it always this cold in late October?" Jacob smiles at his friend's discomfort, something he's rarely witnessed.

Greta comes toward Royce and embraces him. "I'm so glad we've met," she says, a strong breeze playing with her fine chin-length hair. But Jacob hears a thinness in her voice that sounds unconvincing and sees how her body stiffens as she draws away from Royce.

Having made plans for the next day, they wave good-bye. Jacob waits as Royce goes through the sliding door and into the hotel; he closely watches his friend, the jaunty step and the way Royce's shoulders relax as if he's suddenly unburdened, his hand smoothing down his hair. It strikes him that never before has he noted Royce's confident self-satisfaction; he's more or less ignored it. He hears Greta calling him. He turns and sees she has walked ahead to the corner and is about to cross the street. When he catches up to her, he's a little breathless. She asks if Royce will be flying back to Los Angeles on Sunday.

"That's what he's said," Jacob answers, feeling for some reason unsure, wondering when he will see Royce again after this weekend. They meet so infrequently now; more and more he gleans they may not know each other as thoroughly as he thought. It occurs to him he's taken his friendship with Royce for granted. He's always believed he understood him and in turn Royce knew him like no other person had, but now he has his doubts. And there is Catherine too—the missing link, perhaps, between himself and his relationship with Royce. Again he pictures Catherine handing a note to Royce that September night a little over a year ago. But had she? Had he not imagined it, just as he had envisaged Catherine raising her eyebrows as she lay in the hospital bed?

As he and Greta climb the steps to their apartment, Jacob is uneasy; he sees how slowly she ascends, her shoulders thrust back as if she's holding herself together. And he knows in her subtle way she will prick him with one question after another once they are inside. She'll want to know why he had not told her about Royce's stunning resemblance to Tommaso, or that he had lost his sister Catherine only weeks before they met. But he feels justified in his decision not to have been honest with her—first of all, he had not met Tommaso, and although the picture she had shown him of her friend was quite clear, at the same time photos can be deceptive. And in terms of Catherine—how could he have told Greta, someone he hardly knew ten months ago, about something so painful? And most importantly, he had been too numb to do so. Yet despite his rationalizations, he knows by now he should have revealed the truth about when he'd lost Catherine, as well as the possibility there may be a strong likeness between Royce and Tommaso—there had been plenty of time to do so. He shrugs as she opens the door of the apartment. But when she switches on the light in the foyer, his throat feels suddenly dry; he doesn't know how he will answer her. He believes he could lose her over this. How flexible can she be—should she be? She will view it as a matter of trust—a lack of it on his part.

Unbuttoning her coat but not taking it off, she goes directly into the bedroom and sits on the bed. Spreading her hands out on either side of her, she leans back, impassively looks up at him; he's standing on the threshold, and, once their gazes lock, she crosses her legs.

They speak at the same time: "I'm sorry, Greta," he says.

"It's uncanny, the likeness—and Catherine . . . ," she begins thoughtfully.

But he doesn't feel sorry and she knows it, he thinks. In unison again, they speak—she, ironically: "Sorry for what, Jacob?"

He, rationalizing: "I wasn't certain how strong the likeness was; I'd only seen a photo of Tommaso—as you know, I've not met him."

He comes and sits next to her on the bed, takes her hand, squeezes it and says, "I couldn't tell you I had just lost Catherine. I was numb." Her eyes moisten, but he cannot tell if her emotion is one of disappointment or of love.

In a plainspoken way, she asks, "Jacob Printz, are you essentially truthful or naturally evasive?" Taken aback by her words, he studies the outline of her oval face, even, flawless, inherently unreadable, and he isn't certain whether or not she is toying with him. Her brown-gold eyes suddenly clear, she meets his gaze, then looks away.

"Is the resemblance between Royce and Tommaso really uncanny?" he asks softly. "Or was it my imagination? Is it yours? Was I fearful of him resembling Tommaso?"

She laughs, then under her breath says, "You are naive, Jacob. Royce is not personally like Tommaso. And the resemblance is not my imagination." But he hears ambivalence in her tone.

Feeling stung, he puts his hands on her shoulders and she moves toward him as he slips off her coat. Then on her knees, she climbs across the bed and disappears beneath the covers. Soon he follows. Immune to the sound of their coats falling to the floor, they make love, more hungry now, less trusting.

Later, when Jacob awakens, his gaze falls on the clock next to the bed. Only about twenty minutes have passed since he's dozed off. He looks over at Greta; in her sleep she looks neither guileless nor imposing. Her expression is balanced, like a subject in a Gauguin painting, revealing both dispassion and sensuality.

He hears a sound coming from his cell, alerting him that he has received a text. He gets out of bed, searching for his phone—he can't remember where he put it. The bing goes off again and he follows the sound to his coat, lying on the floor at his feet. When he takes the cell from its pocket, he sees the text is from Royce:

> *Need to go back to LA early tomorrow morning—something's come up. Sorry. Hope to see you soon—why don't you and Greta come out to the West Coast. Would love for you to visit.*

After reading Royce's message, Jacob holds the phone in his hand, staring at the words. It occurs to him that maybe Royce intended all along to leave Boston early tomorrow morning. Baffled, he begins to pace in his bedroom. Soon he wanders into the sitting room and pours himself another glass of Malbec. But on the floor next to the chair where Royce was sitting, he notices his friend's briefcase—how battered and old it is.

As he turns toward the light to text Royce, he sees Greta coming into the room, wearing his bathrobe, much too big for her, the belt loosely tied, the knot falling close to her left knee.

"Royce has sent me a text—he needs to go back to Los Angeles, tomorrow morning. I'll let him know about the briefcase," he says, pointing to it. Just as Jacob bends his head to text Royce, the doorbell rings. His gaze follows Greta as she goes to the door of their apartment and then out into the corridor.

"Royce," he hears her say, her voice heavy from sleep, echoing. Soon Royce is standing in their apartment, his hands in his trench coat pockets, his feet spread apart, his head down.

"So you've come for your briefcase. Or is it the briefcase of RJ Waggs?" Jacob says with a weak smile. Noticing Greta's puzzled expression, he explains RJ Waggs is Royce's radio name in Los Angeles. She nods and goes over to the couch and stretches out, her face against the armrest, her eyelids lowering. Before her eyes are fully shut, she looks over at Royce and winces. It seems to Jacob as if she is seeing the resemblance between Royce and Tommaso for the first time all over again. Royce sits in the chair facing the sofa; crossing his legs, he reaches to grasp the handle of the briefcase.

Intuiting that Royce has something of importance to announce, Jacob recalls that day ten years or so ago when playing a one-on-one game of basketball, halfway through they had decided to take a break. Royce, taking a gulp from his water bottle, not looking him in the eye, had told him he'd be moving to the West Coast in a month. Jacob had been taken aback; he'd had no idea his friend had been planning to leave Philadelphia.

Jacob pours a glass of wine for each of them. Greta sits up and curls her legs beneath her. He notices her studying Royce in her impassive way, her eyelids not blinking, as she waits for him to speak.

"I'm not a coward, Jake," Royce says, forcefully.

Now sitting next to Greta, Jacob hears the strain in his friend's voice. "I could not leave without seeing you—though, to be honest, it is what I'd intended to do. To leave you with the briefcase, and disappear, maybe not see you again because maybe you would not want to see me."

"What's inside it, Royce?" Jacob asks abruptly. He watches as Royce takes his hand from the handle of the briefcase and cradles his glass of wine with both palms. In a voice tinged with unexpected sensitivity, Royce begins, "About a year and a half ago, my assistant came into my office and said there was a woman who wanted to see me."

Because of the mellow turn in Royce's tone Jacob feels suddenly calm. It is as if he is in a dark cave, confidently and cautiously feeling his way out, his hands on either wall, his heart steady for now, though ready to beat fiercely if he is no longer able to follow the lone trace of light.

"I asked him if it was someone I knew. He answered that the woman said she knew of me, but had not yet met me and wasn't certain if I knew of her. And we both smiled because most people in the purview of my broadcast know of me, and I may or may not have met them. So there was nothing unusual about that. Then he said she wanted to be interviewed for my 'Tell Me about Your Life' segment." Royce looks over at Greta, then Jacob, explaining it is a previously taped, edited interview with a person who is not a celebrity, someone not known to the public. It is broadcast every Friday afternoon for an hour. The person speaks about his or her life and he, Royce, questions them.

"The ratings are very good for this segment, best of the week." Royce smiles, then continues. "Okay, I told my assistant, I'll tape the interview with her, but she should know I am pretty booked already and so I do not know when it will be aired—maybe not for another six months to a year."

Royce looks directly at Jacob and adds, "Although many people want to be interviewed for this segment, no one before had come directly to my office to inquire about it. And because she did this I was intrigued, and didn't have her go through the usual process of filling out forms, sending them in by email or snail mail and having my assistant read through them, et cetera. I told him to bring her in—I had two or three hours to spare—it was good timing on her part. Not only was I free, I was curious."

His heart now racing, Jacob clasps and unclasps his fingers and soon feels Greta touching his wrist, then grasping his hand. He doesn't look at her, only at Royce, at the movement of his blue-green eyes, like two swift fish, each in a tiny white pond, at his nose, long, straight, uncompromisingly so, and lastly his short, abrupt chin. And it dawns on Jacob that he knows his friend even less than he thought he did a few hours ago.

Royce continues, "She walked in, and we shook hands. I thought she was striking but in an unexpected way—for me, that is—she was dressed in blue jeans, and her hair was pulled away from her face. At first she seemed nervous and told me that before we started taping she wanted to be honest with me—'Full disclosure,' she said and smiled. 'I believe you know my brother, Jake Printz. That is part of the reason I've come to you—I've sort of pieced it together that you are the friend from college he always spoke about, Royce Wagner.'"

"Of course I was surprised by her revelation," Royce says smoothly.

Becoming more and more irritated by Royce's smugness, Jacob longs to strike him. He feels Greta clutching his hand firmly, not letting it go. "Nice introduction, Royce. Get on with it," he says with only a trace of anger, forcing himself not to react. He closes his eyes and takes a deep breath.

Jacob hears Royce continue on in the same voice, as if he is either immune to his distress, or accepting of it. He looks over at Greta and sees how thoroughly she's studying Royce.

"We started taping within ten minutes," Royce says. "She gave her full name and where she was from. I only require a first name, as I like to keep it anonymous as much as I can; people feel more free to talk when their identity is not known. But she chose to reveal who she was. I leaned toward her and asked, as I do all the people I interview, what was her first memory. Most people force themselves to come up with one recollection or another, but she said she had many memories from her childhood, she just didn't know which one came first."

"Don't be so mysterious, Royce," Jacob cries out. "What is it you want me to know about Catherine?"

Royce points to the briefcase and says, "The CDs are in here, Jake—they are for you, the interview never aired. It will never air. I'm giving them to you."

"Were you involved with her or not?" Jacob asks aggressively, knowing with deep sadness that it would be too painful for him to hear his sister's voice—for it would be her voice of the past, and therefore not quite real to him.

"She told me she had just ended a relationship and was not in the mood for another and wouldn't be for a while," Royce said in a clipped voice.

"So then, what is it, Royce?" Jacob asks, his head throbbing. "Why did she move to California?"

Royce smiles and says, "Why do people move out to Los Angeles? Usually it is because they have a dream. Catherine had a dream—she wanted to try to fulfill it, not shy away from it. For instance, she believed your father would have been happier living with a man instead of with your mother—she told me this off the record, of course, over drinks one night—that he, your father, had stifled part of himself, his sexuality, refused to acknowledge it. And so she did not want to hold herself back from what she most desired."

"What was her desire, her dream, Royce?" Jacob asks testily, standing up, instinctively putting up his guard.

"She wanted to sing—mostly the blues, I think. I went to one of her performances. She'd been taking lessons. She was good in sort of a languorous way. She stayed away from social media—she wanted to establish herself first. But I believe she hoped to use her appearance on my show to promote herself—very clever of her, don't you think?"

"You told me on the phone last December that Catherine deserves her privacy, even in death. So why are you here, telling me about her dream, giving me the CDs? What about her so-called privacy?"

Royce shrugs. "I guess I changed my mind. I was thinking more of you now," he says, placing his glass of wine on the floor. Then he gets up from the chair to leave. His mind cloudy, Jacob remains silent, his heart no longer pounding. Soon he hears the door click shut, and is aware of Greta looking up at him, holding his hand as he stands, unwilling to move.

Later in bed, he lies close to Greta; she's sitting up, her back against the headboard, still in his robe. "You didn't tell me about your father," she says, as if mentally adding up the things he hasn't told her. "Did you not know?"

"I wasn't as aware or as certain as Catherine apparently was, but I knew without knowing I knew. It's difficult to describe. It is the same as watching a movie: behind all the dialog and drama you know in an opaque way what the truth is, but you don't fully realize it until the climax, when it is revealed."

"Royce and Catherine were not involved—did you know all along that that was the truth, was that the same as watching a film for you too?"

"Of course he was involved with her—I know Royce," Jacob answers spontaneously. "Or I thought I knew him."

"I don't know, Jacob," Greta says and begins to stroke his head with her long, ringless fingers. "You may be jumping to conclusions. Catherine had a choice to be or not to be involved with him."

Jacob closes his eyes, yearning but not able to believe what she is saying. He wants to tell her, but can't, that Catherine was kind, easily succumbed to people's wishes, yet was fiercely independent as well. He turns his head and looks over at the copy of de Kooning's *Seated Woman* hanging on the wall. Yes, Catherine was both independent and giving—which is what he thinks de Kooning was trying to portray about the figure in this painting. That was the essence of his sister. But when Jacob looks at it again, he realizes it is simply a print of the painting, an impression of who he believes Catherine was; he'll never know for sure. All he can do is cling to this image. Filled with a sudden worry, he wonders why Royce and Catherine had not revealed to him they had met in Los Angeles. Had he been in some way an inadequate friend and brother—was that what had prevented them from telling him? But he can't bring himself to express this deep hurt to Greta. Instead, he says, "I've lost Catherine and Royce—or who I thought Royce was—I can't lose you too, Greta." She continues to calmly stroke his head as he buries his face in her still, scentless breasts, soon wet from his tears.

The following June

Ever since Greta met Royce eight months ago, she has not been able to clearly recall Tommaso—her image of him in front of Titian's *Venus of Urbino,* one she had steadfastly retained, now has been supplanted by one of Royce, sitting in the green-and-white plaid chair, revealing to her and Jacob how he had come to know Catherine. And whenever she looks directly at Tommaso's photo on her phone, she forgets him even more; she is unable to recall his personality, his joie de vivre, often wondering if it is really Royce she is seeing instead. It has crossed her mind that if Tommaso and Royce were standing next to each other, perhaps the resemblance might not be so strong. Maybe she had wished for Royce to look very similar to Tommaso because she had needed him to, just as Jacob had said he might have exaggerated the resemblance out of fear when she had first shown him Tommaso's photo.

With a deep and quiet dismay, she acknowledges that in a sense Tommaso is now dead to her. For has not Royce wiped him from her mind, her experience? In a futile attempt to revive him, every so often she'll take out Tommaso's ring, which she keeps hidden in the bureau drawer with her nightgowns, and will tightly grasp it in her hand, hoping to resurrect her impression of him—but it is to no avail. Yes, all she has is his ring, but she wonders if it really is a family ring—did he find it in an antique store? Is it a copy or a fake? For he never said a word about it to her.

From time to time Greta will also consider returning the ring to Tommaso, but he has not asked her for it. He could reach her, even though she and Jacob are now living in Philadelphia; she hasn't changed her email address, nor her cell number. But on her most cynical days, Greta admits to herself Tommaso has become for her only a name, a nationality, a representative of that nationality. And she wonders if she ever knew him at all. It is as if their relationship—emotional and physical—never existed.

It is an unseasonably hot afternoon in mid-June. Greta gets up from her desk, pulls up the shade, and opens the window; light floods the bedroom, illuminating Jacob's favorite silver pens on the table next to his side of the bed. He's forgotten to bring them with him on his trip to San Francisco. Sitting down again, she opens her computer to check her email. She is surprised to see a message from Elaine—she hasn't heard from her since before she and Jacob left Cambridge six months ago.

As she peruses Elaine's email, she thinks of that late October night in Florence when she had come out of the shower to find Elaine in her room, wearing the high-necked nightgown with pink hearts around the bodice, grasping the bedpost, her eyes steely, and how she'd told Greta she was in love with Tommaso.

In the email Elaine tells her she's finished with her first year of law school, which she found rather disappointing, but she will continue on with it in the fall. And that a few days ago she received a postcard from Beth, who apparently is in Paris with Tommaso. They often go there; it is their home away from home and they hope to remain in the city for most of the summer. They must walk about quite slowly, as the accident has left Tommaso with a limp. Then she adds that Beth has resigned from her position at the college—she has a trust fund, and is convinced that at heart she is more European than American.

As she reads, Greta thinks of the close call she and Jacob had at the café in Paris, and feels a fleeting concern for Beth and Tommaso.

Then she hazily recalls Tommaso talking about coming to America, wanting to see the Liberty Bell. But she no longer remembers where they were when he said it, or how he appeared. Yet how easy it is for her to recall Elaine in her nightgown professing her love for Tommaso. It now strikes her how stoic it had been for Elaine a few weeks later to condone Greta's relationship with Tommaso—she'd been the only one to have known of it.

The image you retain of someone, Greta believes, brings the past, present, and future of a person together for you—yet it is only your perception, your impression of the person. And so isn't your image similar to an inadequate copy?

As Greta ponders how she will answer Elaine's email, her phone rings. It is Jacob. He tells her he will be returning the next morning. He'll be taking a red-eye from San Francisco. He gives her the time and flight number so she will be able to pick him up at the airport. They do not talk long as he has just awakened and sounds groggy. After she clicks off her phone, she feels uneasy. They've been together for eighteen months, yet in certain ways she still does not know him. People have conflicting sides to them, he often says, and you need to get to the center of each person to know the truth. But she does not know his center; he keeps it hidden from her. All she knows is for some reason she and Jacob are not able to part.

She leans forward and begins to type out her response to Elaine's email. She tells her she is now living in Philadelphia, and that she and Jacob are still together. He is no longer teaching, but working as a political adviser. She has been doing temp work and taking graduate classes in museum studies ever since they arrived in Philadelphia in January. She does not say she's realizing more and more that in a certain way a museum is what represents home to her. Nor does she say she no longer remembers much about her time with Tommaso, or that her feelings for Jacob are at times garbled.

When she finishes, she shuts down her computer. Closing her eyes, she tries to imagine Beth and Tommaso walking about the Louvre or the Orsay, museums she had visited with Jacob when they had returned to Paris after the snowstorm. She envisions Beth, wearing a summer halter dress that falls to her knees, a straight cut, a light color, her hair pulled back into a loose ponytail. Though taller than most French women, she is slim, her bone structure more medium than petite. She walks in a meandering way, and Greta imagines her making her way through the Latin Quarter, then on to St-Germain-de-Prés. Yet Greta cannot envisage Tommaso alongside Beth. She tries to remember walking through the Piazza della Signoria or looking at the paintings at the Uffizi with him, but he has become a shadow for her, a block of darkness she cannot permeate because it is without shape and substance. Her frustration mounts.

When she gets up from her desk, she looks out the open window and is met with a strong scent of azaleas coming from the next door neighbor's balcony. The oaks lining the street are still from the heat, the sky a hazy blue. She moves away from the window and goes to her bureau, takes Tommaso's ring out of the drawer, places it on the nightstand next to her bed, shiny and golden in the late morning light. Yes, the Liberty Bell, she thinks.

She leaves the apartment, locks the door, and walks down the street, passing a young couple, holding hands. Greta notices a look of determination crossing the woman's face.

She wonders what Jacob will be like when she picks him up at the airport tomorrow. Will he be the jovial and self-deprecating Jacob, or the nervous and mysterious Jacob? Or the beatific Jacob, like a subject in an El Greco painting? Then there is the practical and slightly cynical Jacob or, more accurately, Jake Printz, a once-upon-a-time campaign operative turned political adviser. It then strikes her that since they've come to Philadelphia, Jacob has not been interested in visiting the museum—she's asked him countless times to go with her. She wonders if he doesn't want to see the de Kooning—he told her after Royce's visit it reminds him so much of Catherine. And at first she was pleased to know the truth, but later vaguely disappointed he had not looked upon it as a homage to their meeting in France. Yet he has not put up the framed print of *Seated Woman* in their Philadelphia home. Instead he has left it in the back of a closet with the battered briefcase containing the three CDs of Catherine's interview—to her knowledge Jacob has not opened the briefcase, nor listened to the recordings. He has shown her a picture of Catherine, one he had kept in his desk at the community college—he's also put this photo in the same closet. Though she has often opened the door to the closet, she stops herself from touching any of these items—it would be a brash invasion of Jacob's privacy.

She thinks of Jacob's parents, whom she has met two or three times over the past six months. Her parents, having had children later in life, are only slightly younger than Jacob's and so she feels comfortable in their presence. Aware of their sadness, she understands their life now, and is always surprised yet touched by their affection for each other. But each time she has noticed Jacob's uneasiness with them, and this confuses her more about Jacob—she feels she knows him less and less. All she can assume is he is this way with them because he blames them for Catherine's death, Greta concludes as she reaches the Liberty Bell Center.

As she stands outside in the long line, she studies the family ahead of her—it might as well be her family as they were twelve or so years ago. The mother is holding the young boy's hand; her expression is even and restrained. The father in blue jeans is restless, pulling his hands in and out of the pockets of his pants, his eyes puffy. The older sister, about sixteen, is dressed in a short skirt, her eyes heavily lined with mascara. And the middle child, like herself, a daughter, standing off a little to the side, intently yet with dispassion studies each member of her family, perhaps wanting more from each of them.

Now inside, Greta approaches the Liberty Bell. It hangs down from a wooden bar. Staring at it, she vividly recalls Tommaso talking about the crack, moving his finger in the air to describe it. Yes, she had loved Tommaso's words, his thoughts—she had loved the idea of Tommaso, and then so shortly afterward she'd been compelled by the reality of Jacob without knowing why. And then she remembers how Tommaso once said you run either toward a ringing bell or away from it. She tries to reach out and touch the Liberty Bell but she is unable to; it is cordoned off. But there is no sound with this bell—it's been silenced because of the crack. And slowly it comes to her:

A cold November night. The Florentine streets, slick from the rain, are filled with people, cars whizzing by. Tommaso, who has been holding her hand, tells her to walk about ten yards ahead of him. And she does so without questioning him. When she believes she's gone the right distance, she turns to look at him. Smiling broadly, he extends his right arm; lifting it over his head, he throws her his gold ring. She easily catches it. When she looks back at Tommaso, she sees a car speeding toward him. She does not move and cannot speak. Shocked. Silenced. Just before he is hit and with a slight tremor in his voice, he cries out, "Run, Greta, run!"

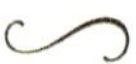

As Jacob boards the plane to Philadelphia he hears one of the flight attendants call another by the name of Catherine. Walking down the aisle to his seat, he turns his head to see who she is. But he is unable to because she's facing away from him. All he can determine is that she is tall and has short, dark hair. He's disappointed, not because he cannot see the flight attendant's face, but because it is a reminder to him that his memory of Catherine is fading. There are times when he'll make it a point to try and recall her, her mannerisms, how she'd say his name. But all he knows for certain is they cared for each other. She is formless now, like a high wispy cloud.

The plane speeds down the runway. As the aircraft ascends, he turns his head to look out the window at the ground below, thinking how pleased he was with the meeting he attended in San Francisco and to be back in the field of a world that is flawed but one he desires. He prefers the role of political adviser—he will be able to maintain his dignity. In his former position he was no more than an able liar, an expert in hyperbole. The goal had been to get votes for your candidate—that was all that mattered—so the senator or governor you represented could implement the ideas they believed in. It was how as a handler you left your influence, your so-called prints on things.

He closes his eyes and pushes back his seat so that he can sleep through the flight. Before dozing off he fleetingly wonders if Greta will be at the airport waiting for him. But he does not dream of Greta. Instead, in his dream:

A great body of water is before him; in the distance, bathed in sunlight, is a long red bridge. Wet from the spray of the waves, his bare feet press into the sand. Suddenly he feels a sharp heaviness in his right hand. When he looks down he realizes he is holding the three CDs he thought were at home, in the briefcase lying on a shelf in the closet. Out of the corner of his eye, he spots the open and empty battered case at the edge of the shore, water lapping into it. He hears the cry of a seagull and gazes upward; there is not one cloud and the sky is the palest of blues. With a deep pain in his heart and the firm resolve and abandon of a discus thrower, he flings the CDs, one by one, into the bay. Then he turns away to step back into his life.

www.ingramcontent.com/pod-product-compliance
Lightning Source LLC
LaVergne TN
LVHW090940080826
845145LV00003B/828

* 9 7 8 0 9 9 9 4 0 0 6 6 1 *